The Elijah Project

# On the Run

Other Bill Myers Books You Will Enjoy

**The Elijah Project**
On The Run
The Enemy Closes In
Trapped by Shadows
The Chamber of Lies

**The Forbidden Doors Series**
The Dark Power Collection
The Invisible Terror Collection
The Deadly Loyalty Collection
The Ancient Forces Collection

**Teen Nonfiction**
The Dark Side of the Supernatural

The Elijah Project

# On the Run

Bill Myers

with James Riordan

*bestselling author*

ZONDER**kidz**

ZONDERVAN.com/
AUTHORTRACKER
*follow your favorite authors*

# For Lee Hough:
## Friend and fellow servant

Zonderkidz

*On the Run*
Copyright © 2009 by Bill Myers

Requests for information should be addressed to:
Zonderkidz, *Grand Rapids, Michigan 49530*

Library of Congress Cataloging-in-Publication Data

Myers, Bill, 1953-
      On the run/ Bill Myers with James Riordan.
         p. cm. -- (Elijah project ; bk. 1)
      Summary: Separated from their parents, sixteen-year-old Zach and his thirteen-year-old sister Piper, with help from two school friends and some divine intervention, try to protect their six-year-old brother from dark forces who know of his supernatural gifts.
      ISBN 978-0-310-71193-3 (softcover)
      [1. Supernatural--Fiction. 2. Christian life--Fiction 3. Healing--Fiction. 4. Adventure and adventurers--Fiction. 5. Brothers and sisters--Fiction. 6. Angels--Fiction. 7. California--Fiction.]
I. Riordan, James, 1936- II. Title.
PZ7.M98234On 2008
[Fic]--dc22

                                            2008001493

Published in association with the literary agency of Alive Communications, Inc., 7680 Goddard Street #200, Colorado Springs CO 80920, www.alivecommunications.com.

*Editor: Jacque Alberta*
*Art direction: Merit Alderink*
*Cover illustration: Cliff Neilsen*
*Interior design: Carlos Eluterio Estrada*

*Printed in the United States of America*

09 10 11 12 13 14 /DCI/ 10 9 8 7 6 5 4

# Table of Contents

"Lo, I am with you always ..."

—Matthew 28:20

# Chapter One

## Beginnings ...

Zach Dawkins headed for the schools.

*Schools*—as in the high school, middle school, and elementary school—that were all lined up side by side on the same street. He called it "Death Row."

Zach was sixteen, with dark hair that stuck out in so many directions it looked like it got cut by a lawn mower gone berserk. It's not that Zach was sloppy, he just had better things to do than worry about his looks, especially when he was late for school ... which was just about every day.

Zach wasn't exactly the responsible type.

Unfortunately, Piper, his thirteen-year-old sister, was.

It seemed her job was to remember everything Zach (and the rest of her family) forgot. Like her brother, she was good-looking (though you couldn't convince her of that). She had beautiful chocolate brown eyes, but you had to work hard to find them beneath all that hair she hid under.

Piper was a bit on the self-conscious side.

At the moment, she was trying to keep up with Zach, while also shouting back to her little brother. "Elijah, come on. Hurry up!"

As usual, six-year-old Elijah dragged behind them. Nothing new there. The guy was always lost in his own world, and he hardly, if ever, talked. Piper loved him fiercely, and she always looked out for him.

But there was no getting around it—the kid was weird.

"Come on," she called. "We're going to be late!"

Elijah nodded, then immediately slowed to watch a butterfly.

Piper blew the hair out of her eyes and stopped with her hands on her hips. "*Elijah ...*" She was about to traipse back and get him, when she heard Zach use that voice he reserved only for making her life miserable.

"Well, well, lookie here."

With a certain dread she turned to her older brother ... and cringed.

Cody Martin, the all-school heartthrob, walked on the other side of the street. He was tall with deep blue eyes and a smile that made it hard for Piper to breathe. Of course he didn't know her from Adam ... or Eve ... but that didn't stop her from pulling up her sweatshirt hood or ducking further under her hair whenever he was around.

Unfortunately, she had stupidly asked her brother about him when the two had played baseball together. And that was all the ammunition Zach needed.

"Look who's across the street," he teased.

"Who?" Piper asked, trying to sound bored. "Oh, you mean Cody. What do I care?"

"Yeah, right," Zach snorted. "So you don't mind if I call him over?"

Suddenly her heart was in her throat. "Zach!"

With a sly grin, he shouted, "Yo, Cody. What's up?"

Cody turned and spotted them. "Hey, Zach." Then, nodding to Piper, he added, "How's it going, Patty?"

"Piper," Zach corrected.

She turned away, whispering between her teeth. "Zach!"

"What?" Cody asked him.

"My sister's name. It's Piper. Actually, it's Naomi Sue, but if you don't want her to beat the tar out of you, I'd stick with Piper."

"Gottcha." Cody grinned.

Zach turned to her and whispered, "So do you want me to call him over?"

"Please, no!" she begged.

"Then you admit you've got a crush on him?"

"No, I just—"

He turned back to Cody and yelled. "So, Cody—"

"Yeah?"

"All right," Piper whispered, "All right, I admit it!"

Zach grinned. "Nothing. Just wondering if you were going to play ball this spring."

"Probably. You?"

"Yeah, probably."

"Cool." Then, spotting a geeky, overweight friend, Cody sped up to join him. "Take care," he turned to say.

"Right," Zach called.

"You too . . . Piper."

Piper's head snapped up to him. The only thing

more startling than hearing him speak her name was the grin he flashed her before moving on.

*He* had *grinned* . . . at . . . *her*.

Suddenly, Piper's hood was up, her hair was down, and her knees were just a little wobbly.

It wasn't until she heard Zach snicker that she came to earth and turned on him. "Is it your goal to be the jerkiest brother on the face of the planet?" she demanded.

Zach laughed. "It's not a goal. It's a duty."

She blew the hair out of her eyes. Looking back to their little brother, she called, "Elijah, *please* hurry!"

Elijah came to attention and ran toward them. That's when Piper noticed the KWIT-TV news van heading up the street.

So did Zach, which explained why he immediately waved and shouted, "Hey, TV news guys! Over here. Check me out. Your next TV star is right here!"

Piper gave another sigh. What was God thinking when he made older brothers?

Suddenly, she noticed a small cocker spaniel puppy running into the street in front of them. It was followed by a little girl, probably in kindergarten.

Neither of them saw the car coming from the opposite direction.

"Watch it!" Piper shouted.

The little girl looked up, but it was too late.

The driver hit the brakes, tires screeching. The car's right front wheel ran over the dog with a sickening *K-THUMP* while the front bumper hit the little girl. It knocked her hard to the ground, causing the back of her head to slam onto the concrete.

Neither the girl nor the dog moved.

The driver opened the car door, his mouth hanging open in shock and horror. The crossing guard, who had seen the whole thing, ran toward them. The news van jerked to a stop as the woman reporter leaped out of the still-rolling vehicle.

"Get the camera rolling!" she called over her shoulder.

"I'm on it!" the cameraman shouted just behind her.

Students quickly gathered, pressing in around the car and little girl. By the time Zach and Piper arrived, the crossing guard was already shouting, "Stand back! Give her air! Everybody, stand back!"

Piper glanced around for her little brother, but he was nowhere to be found.

"Elijah?" she called. "Elijah?"

She turned to Zach but he was too busy trying to get a look at the girl to pay attention.

"Elijah!"

The news crew pushed past them for a closer shot.

"Hey, check it out," the reporter pointed. But she wasn't pointing at the little girl. She had noticed something across the crowd and on the other side of the street.

Piper followed her gaze to see ... Elijah.

He sat on the curb holding the dead puppy. But instead of crying, his lips quietly moved—almost like he was whispering to it. And then, to Piper's dismay, the puppy began to move. A little at first, but it soon began wiggling, squirming, and even lifting up its head to lick Elijah's face.

"Did you get that?" the reporter cried.

"I've got it!" the cameraman shouted.

"It's like he healed it or something!" she exclaimed.

With a grin, Elijah set the dog down. It began jumping and running around like it had never been hurt.

"Get in closer," the reporter ordered. "I'm going to talk to him."

Only then did Piper realize what she had to do. "Elijah!" She brushed past the reporter and raced for her little brother. "Elijah, come on!"

The little boy looked up, grinning even bigger.

"Excuse me?" the reporter called from behind her. "May I ask you a few questions?"

Piper ignored her. "Come on little guy," she said as she arrived. She put her hand on his shoulder, looking for a way to get out of there. "Mom and Dad won't like this. Not one bit."

"Excuse me!" the reporter shouted.

Spotting the school, Piper figured it was better than nothing, and started toward it. "Let's go."

"Excuse me?"

They walked faster.

"Excuse me!"

They started to run, neither turning back.

●

Judy Dawkins was struggling with the vacuum cleaner when her husband burst through the front door.

She looked up, startled. Seeing the concern on his face, she asked, " What's wrong?"

He tried to smile, but something was up.

"Mike, what is it?"

He walked over to the TV remote. Without a word, he snapped it on and found the news. Finally, he spoke. "They've been playing this all morning."

A white-haired anchorman addressed the camera: "Carly Tailor, our Newsbeat reporter, is still on the scene. Carly?"

A young woman appeared on the screen. She stood

perfectly poised in front of the news van. "Thank you, Jonathan. As we've been saying, something very strange happened over on Walnut Boulevard this morning. Let's roll the footage, please."

The scene cut to an accident sight where medics loaded a little girl into an ambulance.

The reporter continued. "At approximately eight o'clock this morning, LeAnne Howard ran into the street after her dog and was struck by an oncoming car. From there she was taken to St. Jerome's Hospital where her condition is reported as critical. There is speculation that she will shortly be transported to the Children's Surgical Unit at Eastside Memorial. But there is another side to this story that we found most interesting ..."

The scene cut to a cocker spaniel lying in front of a car.

"This footage was taken immediately after the accident. As you can see, the dog looks ... well, it looks dead ... or at least severely injured."

Again the picture changed. This time a little boy sat on the curb holding the dog and whispering to it.

"Oh no," Mom brought her hand to her mouth. "It's Elijah!"

The reporter continued. "But moments later, as people were trying to help the girl, this small boy picked up her dog and ... you'll have to see for yourself. This is simply unbelievable."

Tears filled Mom's eyes as she watched the dog suddenly sit up in Elijah's lap and then lick his face.

"That's amazing," the anchorman said. "Let's see it again."

While the scene replayed, the reporter continued. "We tried to interview the boy, but a girl, the girl you see here, rushed him away."

Mom stared at the screen as Piper appeared and hurried Elijah away from the camera and toward the school.

The report continued, but Mom no longer heard. Tears blurred her eyes as her husband wrapped his arm around her.

"Don't cry, sweetheart," he said. "We knew this day would happen, didn't we?"

She tried to answer, but her throat was too tight with emotion.

Dad repeated the words more softy. "Sooner or later we knew it would happen."

●

Monica Specter and her two male assistants sat in the dingy, cockroach-infested hotel, staring at the same newscast.

With a sinister grin, she switched off the television. "All right team, the objective's been sighted." She rose and started for the adjacent room. "Pack up. We're leaving in fifteen minutes."

Bruno answered. He was a hulk of a man whose neck was as thick as most people's thighs and whose upturned nose looked like he'd run into a brick wall as a child (several times). "Uh ... okay. Where are we goin'?"

Monica stopped, flipped aside her bright red hair, and stared at him in disbelief. "Westwood, you dolt. You saw the news. The boy we're tracking is in Westwood."

Bruno nodded. "Uh ... right."

She looked at him another moment. Then, shaking her head, she disappeared into the other room.

Silas, their skinny partner with a long, pointed nose,

shut down his laptop. "You shouldn't ask stupid questions like that," he said to Bruno.

Bruno nodded, then stopped. "But how do I know they're stupid if I don't ask 'em?"

Silas sighed. "Because you're going to try something brand new."

"What's that?"

"You'll try thinking before you speak."

Bruno frowned, not completely sure he understood the concept. Then summoning up all his brain cells, he answered, "Huh?"

Silas answered. "We've been looking for this kid eight months now—checking newspaper articles, surfing the Net—and then, out of the blue, he suddenly winds up on TV?"

Bruno grinned. "Yeah, some coincidence, huh?"

"Yeah, right. That was no coincidence."

"You think Shadow Man had something to do with it?"

Silas shrugged. He never liked talking about the head of their organization. To be honest, the man gave him the willies.

"Come on," he said, changing the subject. "Let's get packed and grab the kid."

# Chapter Two

## On the Run

Mom furiously threw clothes into each of her three children's suitcases.

They'd been discovered. Found out. And in a matter of time they'd be taken. But not all of them, just one.

Just Elijah.

She heard car tires screech outside. She raced to the bedroom window to see a strange trio leap out of a green van and start down the sidewalk. First, there was a red-headed woman. Somehow she had learned the delicate art of stomping in high heels. Behind her was a giant of a man. And, last but not least, was a skinny, short man with a long, pointed nose ... who was carrying a gun!

"Honey!" her husband shouted as he raced up the stairs.

"I see them," she called.

He entered the room. "We'll have to draw them off."

"As decoys?"

He nodded. "I'll leave a note. The kids can meet up with us tonight."

"Oh, Mike ..." Once again, tears filled her eyes.

"It's the only way, sweetheart." His own voice thickened with emotion. "For now, it's all we can do."

●

Monica sent Bruno to the back of the house while she and Silas knocked at the front door.

There was no answer.

She knocked harder.

Repeat in the no-answer department.

She turned to Silas. "You may have to break it in."

Silas squirmed. "I'm not the break-down-the-door guy. That's Bruno's department." Suddenly he brightened. "But I'll be happy to shoot off the lock if you want."

Monica gave him a look.

It's not that Silas was a gun nut; he just had this thing about blowing things up first and asking questions later. The worst was the time Bruno brought home a battery-operated puppy for Monica's birthday. (It really wasn't her birthday, but it was the thought that counted. Actually, in Bruno's case it wasn't the thought, either, since thoughts were not exactly something he specialized in.)

Anyway, once Monica rejected the gift (she always rejected Bruno's gifts), Bruno pretended it was *his* birthday. After a rousing chorus of "Happy Birthday to Me," he unwrapped the toy.

"Oh, what a wonderful surprise," he shouted.

Next came the hard part—figuring out how to put the batteries in. Once he accomplished that, Bruno turned on the toy and let it loose on the floor. Immediately, the mechanical puppy began prancing around and barking.

Silas, who was trying to watch a baseball game on TV, wasn't impressed.

"Will you turn that thing off?" he demanded. "I'm watching the game!"

"Oh, sorry," Bruno said.

But before he could turn it off he had to catch it. And since the only thing worse than Bruno's brain function was his coordination, he was never quite able to apprehend the crafty little toy.

"Turn it off!" Silas shouted.

"I'm trying, I'm trying," Bruno said.

Finally, Silas saved him the effort.

The first shot sent the mechanical puppy into the air.

The second blew its little head off.

The third turned it into a pile of gears, fake fur, and a warranty label they somehow suspected was no longer valid.

Yes, Silas definitely had a thing about blowing stuff up.

Back at the house, the garage door behind them began to rise. Monica spun around to see a blue Jeep Cherokee backing out.

"They're trying to get away!" she cried.

They took off for the garage but were too slow. The car barreled backward down the driveway and onto the road, where it skidded to a stop. Then, with tires squealing, it peeled out and zoomed up the street.

"Get 'em!" Monica screamed as she turned for their van.

Unfortunately, Silas didn't turn as quickly as she did, which meant he crashed into her ... and fell onto the driveway ... where they got tangled up together.

After flopping around a bit, Silas finally pulled his foot out of her purse, and she pulled her arm out of his shirt. At last they scrambled to their feet and raced for the van.

"Don't let them get away!"

●

As they headed home from school, Zach was his usual irritating self.

"So you're a big TV star now," he teased.

"What?" Piper asked.

"Couple kids saw it at lunch—you and Elijah were all over the news."

"Great," Piper sighed. "Mom and Dad aren't going to like that."

Zach nodded. "It's not exactly the low profile they tell us to keep."

Piper threw a look over her shoulder to Elijah, who was his usual fifty steps behind. This time he'd been stopped by three older kids.

"Hey, it's miracle boy," one of them taunted.

"Yeah," another said. "How 'bout doing a trick for us, Freako?"

Without thinking, Piper launched into her attack mode. It made no difference that there were three of them and one of her, or that their backs were to her so she didn't know how tough they were.

The point is, they were going after Elijah, so she was going after them.

"Leave him alone!" she shouted.

She grabbed the nearest kid who had just arrived. She spun him around only to see that it was ... Cody.

"Hey ... uh, Piper."

She swallowed then croaked, "Leave my brother alone!"

"Right, I was just—"

"You heard me!"

"I know, that's what I was telling—"

"I don't care how gorgeous you think you are, you don't mess with my brother!"

She pulled up her sleeves and glared at the other two boys like she was ready for a fight. They exchanged nervous looks, as if they were dealing with a crazy person.

"That goes for you too!"

Not wanting to tangle, particularly with a crazy person, they backed away. Then they turned and sauntered off. They fired off the expected insults, but Piper didn't care. She'd made her point. No one messed with her little brother.

It was about this time that she noticed Elijah tugging on her sleeve. She turned to him. "What?"

He pointed to Cody and shook his head.

"What?" she repeated.

Cody coughed slightly and explained, "I think he's telling you I was trying to help."

"Wh ... what?" She looked to Cody, then back to Elijah, who nodded broadly.

"Those two goons were giving him a rough time, so I came over to—"

"Hey, Cody," Zach strolled up to them. "I see Holster and Larson were trying to be tough guys again."

"Yeah," Cody agreed. "They'll never learn."

Zach nodded. "Looks like you scared them off."

"Actually, I think Piper did most of the scaring."

All three turned to Piper, whose ears were suddenly burning red hot. "You ... you were trying to help? She stammered. "I thought—"

"Yeah, I figured," Cody said. He flashed her that killer grin.

Piper tried to answer, but it's pretty hard talking with your jaw hanging open.

Cody cranked up his grin even brighter. "Don't sweat it. Truth is, I like people who stand up for others. *A lot.*"

Piper may have nodded. She wasn't sure. All she knew was that her mouth was still hanging open (and she was praying there was no drool).

"Maybe I can give you a call sometime?" he asked. "I mean if you don't mind."

If her jaw was hanging open before, it was dragging on the ground now.

"Piper?"

She tried moving her mouth, but nothing happened.

He spoke again. "Piper?"

"Uh-huh," she heard herself croak.

"If I'm going to call you ... I'll need your cell number."

"Uh-huh."

He paused, waiting. Was it her imagination or was his friendly smile turning into a look of pity?

At last, Zach came to her rescue. "It's 484–1601, right, Pipe?"

"Uh-huh."

"Great." Cody grabbed a pen and wrote it on the back of his hand.

"Thanks for helping out," Zach said. "With Elijah, I mean."

"No prob." Cody answered as he turned and started up the sidewalk.

Piper wasn't sure how long she stood there. All she remembered was Zach putting his arm around her shoulder and easing her in the direction of their house.

"Come along now," he said gently. "Everything will be all right."

•

Mom and Dad sped down the entrance ramp and merged onto the freeway. The green van was close behind ... and getting closer by the second.

"They're closing in," Dad said, looking in the rearview mirror.

"Can we outrun them?" Mom asked.

"I doubt it. But we can stay ahead of them long enough for the kids to see the note and get away."

•

"What happened?" Piper said as they stood in the middle of the kitchen. The vacuum cleaner was out, unwashed dishes sat in the sink, and the floor was covered with clothes from the dryer.

"Looks like they were in a hurry," Zach said as he opened the fridge to get some milk.

"Thank you, TV news!" Piper drolled. "They also left the garage door open."

Grabbing a dirty glass from the sink, Zach asked, "You don't think anything serious could have happened, do you?"

Piper cringed as he poured the milk into the filthy glass.

He looked at her. "What?"

She started to explain and then stopped. With Zach it would do no good.

Elijah spotted a note on the counter. Silently, he scooped it up and handed it to Piper.

"What's that?" Zach asked between gulps.

"It's from Mom and Dad," Piper said. She began reading:

*"No time to explain. Meet us at Aunt Myrna's tonight. Take everything you need in case we can't come back."*

Zach stopped drinking. "Can't come back?"

"Oh no," Piper groaned. "It's happening again, isn't it?"

Zach frowned. "Maybe ... but Aunt Myrna's all the way in Pasadena. We don't even know her address."

Piper tapped the note. "It's right here."

"Anything else?"

"Just a Bible verse." Since they were kids, Mom and Dad always ended their notes with a verse from the Bible.

Zach finished the milk and belched. "Which one?"

Piper read the verse:

*"'Lo, I am with you always ...'* Matthew twenty-eight, verse twenty."

"That's it?" Zach asked.

"Almost." Piper swallowed. "There's one last word."

"Which is ...?"

*"Hurry!"*

●

Monica Specter squinted through the dirty windshield as Silas drew closer to the Jeep.

"I don't see no kids in there," Bruno called from the backseat.

"Neither do I," Silas said. Turning to Monica, he asked, "Should I force them off the road?"

Silas liked crashing into cars as much as he liked blowing up battery-operated puppies. Unfortunately, Monica had a better idea.

Unfortunately, because the last thing in the world she wanted to do was put a call in to her boss. He was creepy. And not as in a little weird. He was creepy as in A LOT WEIRD.

Maybe it was his voice—the way it sort of slithered around your mind and hissed in your ears. Slithered and hissed the way rattlesnakes do.

Or maybe it was his tremendous size. He wasn't a little overweight, he was REALLY OVERWEIGHT. Picture Jabba the Hutt from *Star Wars*. Yeah, that was pretty close to his size.

Actually, neither his voice nor his weight was a problem compared to his face. The reason? She never saw it. Well, it was there and everything, stuck on top of his neck like everyone else's. But she could never quite make it out. It always seemed to lurk and hide in shadows. Even in the brightest light, she still couldn't see his face.

In any case, despite all these lovely reasons she didn't want to call, she knew the time had come. Whether she liked it or not, she knew what she had to do.

Monica took a deep breath, reached into her purse for her cell phone, and began to dial.

●

The office was black. Not black as in dark with no lights, but black as in all black—black carpet, black desk, black phones. Even the pens and paper clips were black.

The phone rang only once before a shadowy form reached over and picked it up.

"Yesss," it hissed in a strange, quivering voice.

"Got them in sight, sir," Monica said over the phone. "But I'm not sure the kid is with them."

"What?!" the dark form demanded.

"We're coming up on Lankersham Boulevard. Should we force them off the road?"

"Leave that to me. I shall contact otherssss."

"But—"

"Just find the boy!"

"Yes, sir," Monica said.

Without another word, the shadow creature slammed down the phone.

●

"They're peeling off," Dad called as he looked through the mirror.

Mom turned to see the green van taking the exit ramp behind them. "Do you think they've given up?" she asked.

He said nothing, and she turned to him. The weary expression on his face said more than she wanted to know.

They drove in silence through the traffic—five, ten minutes—lost in their own thoughts, recalling memories of how time after time they had to pull up stakes and leave. In the early days, they'd tried going to the police. But what could they tell them? That their son had been born with strange gifts? That there was an organization connected to a dark, sinister force that would stop at nothing to get their hands on him?

Not exactly the type of thing police would believe.

Dad slowed the Jeep, and Mom looked up as they came to a stop.

"What's wrong?" she asked.

"Looks like an accident ahead. An overturned truck or something."

She nodded and returned to her thoughts. Even before he was born, she knew Elijah was different. To this day, she remembered the crazy man on the street who stopped her when she was pregnant. The one who started telling her all the things her baby would do and how he was even mentioned in the Bible. Then there was the—

The banging on the Jeep window jarred Mom from her thoughts. She spun around to see a good-looking man in a suit.

He motioned for her to roll down the window.

Throwing a look to Dad, who nodded, she reached for the button and rolled it down.

"Hello, there," he said in a thick Australian accent. "Leave everything and walk away with me. We've got a car waiting on the other side of the freeway."

"Who ... who are you?" Dad demanded.

"Oh, I think you know who we are, mate. Now come on."

"You just can't grab us in the middle of traffic!"

"Of course I can. That is if you want to see your children alive again."

Mom froze. "Our children? What have you done with the children?!"

"There's only one way to find out." He turned and walked away from the car.

Mom twirled to her husband. "What do we do?"

He frowned.

"Maybe it's a bluff," she said. "Maybe the kids are safe."

"Maybe ..." Dad let out a heavy sigh. "But is that a risk we're willing to take?"

She looked at him a moment then shook her head. Then they both reached for the door handles and exited the car.

"Elijah …" Piper looked down into her little brother's suitcase. "You can't take all this stuff! The lid won't close."

He crossed his arms and scowled.

"Sorry, buddy."

She began pulling things out. First went the photos. Not just those from his room, but also from the hallway, the mantle, next to Mom's bed, and on Dad's dresser.

"Didn't you pack any clothes?" she asked.

He scowled harder and pointed at the shirt, pants, and shoes he was wearing.

"You have to pack more than those."

He lifted up his shirt to show his underwear.

Piper smiled and reached back into the suitcase. The next thing she pulled out was a heavy book—the family Bible. He loved that thing. And even though he couldn't read, he'd stare at the printed pages for hours. He especially liked the last section, the book of Revelation.

Piper continued to dig.

This was their fourth move in six years. And, like the others, it was always last minute with no explanation. When they tried to get their parents to tell them why, the answer was always the same: "When you're older we'll explain. Right now, the less you know the better it will be."

Piper blew the hair out of her eyes. It wasn't anything illegal, she knew that. The family always went out of their way to do the right thing. So what could it be?

She looked back into the suitcase and pulled out Zach's baseball card collection. Next she felt warm fur and pulled out her koala bear—the one she'd slept with since she was a baby. She'd wanted to pack it in her own suitcase but didn't have room.

"Oh, Eli," she said softly. "That is so sweet. But you have to pack something for your—"

She was interrupted by Zach shouting from downstairs. "Looks like we've got company!"

She moved to the window with Elijah. Sure enough, a green van had pulled up and the door now slid open. The first person to step out was a skinny man with a funny nose . . . and a gun.

That's all Piper needed to see.

"Come on, Eli," she whispered. "Let's get out of here."

"The back door!" Zach called. "Let's sneak out and head across old lady Hagen's yard!"

●

Monica was surprised to see the front door unlocked. Instead of breaking it down (or allowing Silas to shoot it) she simply pushed it open, and they walked inside.

She turned to the men. "Bruno, check the back door. Silas, look upstairs."

They nodded and went to work, just as Monica's cell phone rang. She flipped it open and answered, "Hello."

"We have the parentsss," the voice hissed through the phone. "You were correct. The children are not with them."

Monica nodded as she moved through the kitchen. "It doesn't look like they're here, either."

"You have lossst them?" the voice hissed, sounding even darker than before.

Monica spotted a note on the counter and silently read it:

*No time to explain. Meet us at Aunt Myrna's tonight. Take everything you need in case we can't come back.*

*"Lo, I am with you always . . ." — Matthew 28:20*

At the bottom was an address.

"No, sir, I haven't lost them." Monica's thin lips curled into what was a cross between a snarl and a smile. "In fact, I know right where they're going."

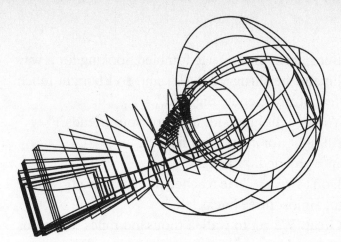

# Chapter Three

## A Close Call

Zach lugged Eli's suitcase and his own down the sidewalk.

Piper pulled hers on little attached wheels. When she'd picked it out with Mom, she'd known the wheels were a good, efficient feature.

Piper had a thing about being "efficient."

"I wish Dad would've left us some money for a cab," she said with a sigh. "The bus will take forever."

"Actually," Zach explained, "he probably figured we had enough."

"Why's that?"

"He gave me a bunch of money for football equipment and stuff, but I ..." Zach came to a stop.

Piper turned to him. "But you what?"

"But I, well, um ..." He fumbled, looking for a way out. Finally, he shrugged. "All right, so I bought lunch for a few of my friends. Big deal."

"You bought lunch for a few of your friends?!"

"All right, for *a lot* of my friends."

Piper groaned. "Zach ..."

"Don't sweat it." He reached into his pocket. "We've still got almost three bucks left."

"Great. We get to walk a thousand miles to the bus stop, then ride the smelly thing all the way across town just so you could be B.M.O.C."

"Big Man on Campus?" Zach asked.

Piper shook her head. "Big Moron on Campus."

Elijah began tugging on Zach's sleeve.

"What is it, little buddy?"

Elijah pointed at a sign that read *Hospital*, with an arrow pointing down the street.

"You want to go to the hospital?" Zach said.

"Are you feeling sick?" Piper asked in sudden concern.

Elijah shook his head.

"Sorry, pal," Zach said. "No field trips today. We gotta keep moving. Hey, there's the bus now."

"Yeah," Piper agreed. "I can smell it from here."

Piper didn't dislike riding buses, per say. It was more like a deep hatred, a powerful loathing. In short, she despised it with every bone in her body.

It wasn't just the smelly exhaust, the sticky seats, or the sweet old ladies that always wound up sitting next to her and talking her ears off. The loathing went deeper, and it had started a long time ago. When she was seven, to be exact. That's when little Billy Hutton thought it would be great fun to sit behind her on the school bus and play "flick the girl's ears."

Yes, sir, lots of fun ... at least for the first couple days. But after a week or two it got a little boring—and painful. So, after asking him to stop for the hundredth time and complaining to the bus driver for the hundredth and one time, little Piper took matters into her own hands.

Translation: She leaped over the seat and beat the tar out of him.

Billy didn't laugh much after that. It's too embarrassing to laugh when you've been beaten up by a girl. (Even more embarrassing to laugh when you no longer have front teeth because of it.)

Of course, Mom and Dad weren't fond of paying for the dental bills. And Piper was even less fond of them taking it out of her allowance for the next thousand years. But Billy never showed interest in her again.

Unfortunately, neither did any of the other boys.

Ever.

●

Monica sat in the passenger seat of the green van looking for any sign of the kids.

"They can't be too far," she grumbled. "They're on foot."

Silas nodded from behind the wheel and turned the van up another street. A block later they came to a stoplight.

"There they are!" Bruno shouted from the backseat.

"Where?" Monica demanded.

"Across the street! At the bus stop!"

"Great." Silas grinned.

"And there's the bus!" Monica pointed.

Silas looked up the street and saw the approaching bus. It was half a block away. "No problem," he said. "We've got plenty of time to get over there and grab them before it gets here."

The light changed, and he started to make a U-turn to cross the street when, suddenly, a homeless man appeared in front of them.

Silas slammed on the brakes. "Hey!"

The man didn't move.

Silas blasted the horn. "HEY!"

The homeless man looked up and smiled.

Silas blew the horn again. "Get out of the way!"

The man raised a hand to his ear as if he couldn't hear.

"The bus is coming!" Monica yelled.

"Come on, pal!" Silas shouted, motioning for him to move.

"Hurry!" Monica cried.

"What can I do?!" He hit the horn again.

The bus entered the intersection and pulled to a stop in front of the kids.

"They're getting on!" Monica yelled.

Silas continued honking. The man continued smiling.

"Run over him!" she shrieked.

With a belch of black smoke, the bus began to pull off.

"They're getting away!" Monica banged on the dashboard. "They're getting away!"

Silas turned back to the homeless man ... only to discover he was no longer there. "Where'd he go?"

"Who cares?" Monica screamed. "Follow that bus!"

Silas resumed the U-turn, only to have another car pull out in front of him. Again he slammed on the brakes, and again he blasted the horn.

But the car wouldn't move. Actually, it couldn't move. The homeless man had crossed the street and now blocked the traffic coming from the opposite direction.

"Unbelievable," Silas said with a sigh as he watched the bus head off down the road.

"Now what do we, uh, do?" Bruno called from the backseat.

"We meet them at their aunt's," Monica said. She pulled out the note she'd picked up from the counter. "If we can't grab them here, we'll grab them there."

Silas nodded. When the traffic finally cleared, he hit the gas. He drove like a madman to make sure they arrived before the kids.

Thirty minutes later, they pulled up in front of the aunt's house.

"You guys wait here," Monica said as she opened the van's door.

"Don't you want us to go with you?" Silas asked.

"Yeah, you might need, like, a protector or somethin'," Bruno said.

Monica looked at him for a long moment. For weeks she figured Bruno had been getting a crush on her. And now, by the way he tried to suck in his gut, grin, and smooth down his hair all at the same time, she was sure of it.

Finally she spoke. "I don't want any trouble here."

"Gotcha." Bruno grinned. Both he and Silas reached for their doors.

"No, listen to me," Monica said. First she pointed at Silas. "Too creepy looking." Then she pointed at Bruno. "Too stupid."

They both stared.

"Understand?"

The big guy looked down and nodded. He seemed to wilt before her very eyes.

She continued. "Just wait here for me."

Neither answered.

With a heavy sigh, she stepped out of the van and closed the door behind her.

Quickly, she hurried up the walk. As she arrived at the door, she took a compact from her purse and checked her face in the mirror. She tried smiling to soften her hardness. But no matter how she smiled, her face always looked as strained as a tortoise with a migraine.

She finally gave up and rang the bell.

A kind, older woman with silver hair opened the door. "Yes?"

Monica tried her best to look pleasant. "Are you ... Myrna?" she asked, suddenly realizing she didn't know Aunt Myrna's last name.

But Myrna saved her. "Dawkins. Yes, I am."

Monica tried smiling again. Her attempt to smile caused her physical pain. "I'm sorry to have to tell you this, but your brother's family was in a car accident up north. They're at Bellevue Hospital in Ventura."

"Oh no!" Aunt Myrna cried. "Are they all right?"

"It's too early to tell. I'm friends with your sister-in-law. She wanted me to ask you to come to the hospital right away."

Aunt Myrna nodded. "Thank you, thank you." She turned and called up the stairs to her husband. "Tom! We've got to go to Ventura right now! Mike's family has been in an accident!"

Thanking Monica once again, she shut the door.

Monica sneered in contentment as she headed back to the van.

"Any luck?" Silas called from the window.

She nodded and climbed inside. "Park down the block, in a place where we can watch the house without being spotted."

Silas dropped the car into gear. But as they pulled away, Bruno let out a forlorn sigh with a couple sniffles.

Monica turned and asked, "What's the matter with you?"

Silas explained. "He's upset because you said he was stupid."

Monica turned back to Bruno and said in her most comforting and understanding voice, "Bruno ... dear, dear Bruno?"

He looked up, hopefully. "Ye ... yes?" he answered between sniffles.

"Knock it off!"

●

After three bus transfers (and more than a little complaining from Piper), the kids finally approached their destination. Or so they hoped.

"You sure you remember how to get there?" Piper asked Zach for the hundredth time.

And for the hundredth time, Zach sighed. "Sure I'm sure. Their house is just down the street from that park."

"Which park is that?"

Zach shrugged. "You know, the park."

Piper looked at him.

"What?" he asked.

"Can I see the note please?"

"What note?"

"The one with the address."

"Oh, that note." Zach reached into his shirt pocket, but only found a flyer for some concert. He checked his back pocket. It was his history assignment. He tried his left pocket and found ... two one-dollar bills ... and forty cents in change.

Piper looked at him in disbelief.

He tried his right pocket and found two pieces of gum and half an eraser.

Piper rolled her eyes.

"What?" he repeated.

"You lost the note?"

"What do I need a stupid note for? Her place is on Jasmine Drive, just down from the park."

*"Which* park?" she repeated.

"How should I know? I mean, how many parks can there be in the city?"

Just then, the bus slowed as the driver called out, "Rutherford Park. Next stop, Cantrell Park, followed by Gelford Park."

If looks could kill, Zach would be making funeral arrangements for himself.

Suddenly, Eli leaped to his feet and pointed out the window toward a large statue of a horse.

"This is it!" Zach cried. "The park with the horse!"

"Are you sure?" Piper asked.

"Sure I'm sure!"

Seconds later, all three piled out of the bus and headed down the street toward Aunt Myrna's.

"I'm starved," Zach said. "I hope she's got dinner for us."

Piper gave another one of her world-famous sighs. "I'd just settle for a hug. Do you think we'll go back home tonight?"

Zach shrugged. "I doubt it. Remember the last time we had to move?"

"How could I forget? It was in the middle of the night."

"Yeah," Zach said. "We had to keep the TV on so people would think we were still there watching it."

"And you wanted it to be on some stupid football game."

"Well, it was better than your America's Top whatever it was."

"It was the middle of spring, Zach. They don't play football in the spring."

"Details, details."

Piper gave up on sighing and tried one of world-famous eye rolls. She still remembered that night vividly. Once they had decided on the TV show, an old *CSI* rerun, they had to push the car out of the garage without turning on the lights ... or the engine. It was suppose to be so no one would hear them leaving. And, for the most part, they were pretty successful—except for the part of Zach pushing the car by holding on to the steering wheel. Actually, that wasn't the problem. It was the horn on the steering wheel. The horn he accidentally pressed again and again, and again some more. The horn that managed to wake up the entire neighborhood and made every dog in the city begin barking.

So much for silence. Maybe that's why this time Mom and Dad decided to leave without their help.

"Anyways," Zach said, bringing her back to the present. "I'm betting it's the same thing now. You know, them having to leave at the last minute."

"Why won't they ever tell us what's happening?" Piper complained.

He gave another shrug. "You know what they say—we're better off not knowing. At least for now."

She nodded and looked back to Elijah. She knew there was a connection between their sudden moves and her little brother, but what?

Suddenly, her cell phone—which Zach had programmed for her—rang to the tune of "If I Only Had a Brain," from *The Wizard of Oz.*

She pulled the phone from her pocket and checked the caller ID. It read *Out of Area.* She flipped it open and anxiously answered. "Hello, Mom?"

"No, it's Cody," the voice replied.

Her heart sank and swelled at the same time. "Uh … hi," she stammered.

"So, what're you up to?" he asked.

She swallowed nervously. The last thing she wanted to do was cut him off, but she didn't have much choice. "Listen … Cody. Now's not such a good time. We're kinda busy and—"

"Where are you?" he asked. "I dropped by your place, but nobody was home."

"Yeah … we're on the way to my aunt's in Pasadena. We took the bus."

"The bus!" Cody exclaimed. "All the way out there? Where are your folks?"

Zach pointed across the street. "There's the house."

"Uh, listen, Cody …" Just saying his name made her mouth dry. "I'm sorry, but I really gotta go. I'll talk to you later."

"Yeah, sure, but—"

Piper cringed as she closed her phone on him.

"Where's Dad's car?" Zach asked.

"Maybe …" She cleared her throat. "Maybe he went to get pizza. We always have pizza when we come here."

They moved across the street and up to the front door. Zach knocked and waited. Piper blew the hair from her eyes and reached over to ring the bell.

A moment later, the door swung open. The woman standing before them was in her thirties with long red hair and a strangely forced smile. "Hello. You must be Mike and Judy's children."

Zach and Piper exchanged looks.

"I'm ... Elaine, a house guest of your Aunt Myrna's. They went to pick up some dinner." She opened the door wider. "Won't you come in? They'll be back anytime."

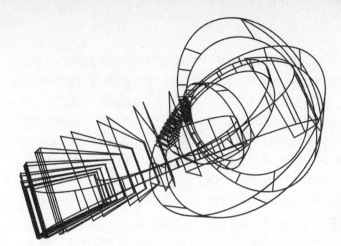

# Chapter Four

## Extra Sausage

Cody stared at his cell phone. "She hung up on me."

Willard, his geeky, overweight friend, replied, "Perhaps she is too enamored of your fabled charm to speak directly to you."

Cody frowned. "And what would that mean in English ...?"

Willard translated. "Maybe she thinks you're too hot."

Cody shook his head. "Don't be stupid."

Willard smiled to himself. Cody was the best friend a guy could have. Thoughtful, modest, and always there when the chips were down. But when it came to girls, he was clueless. The guy had absolutely no concept of his incredible looks or the effect he had on girls ... which is probably why they were all nuts over him.

Willard remembered the time in third grade when they were playing dodgeball and two girls were chosen to be captains. To say that they were each crazy to get Cody on their team was an understatement. To say that it involved screaming, a fist fight, and huge clumps of pulled-out hair on the gym floor when they were through was the least of it.

The fact that Willard was always chosen last was another truth. But one he was used to.

At the moment the two of them were working in Willard's dad's garage, tinkering on Willard's latest invention. In the past he had created other mind-numbing devices:

ROCKET-POWERED BOWLING BALLS—a lot of fun, except for the holes they put in the back walls of bowling alleys.

MAKE-YOU-INVISIBLE ELECTRON BEAMS—a useful invention, except it only worked on skin and muscle, leaving folks walking around like human skeletons (not one of human kind's more attractive features).

Finally, there was the ever-popular AUTOMATIC HAIR CURLER—a hit with the girls, except that it fried their hair and made them permanently bald.

Now Willard was working on his latest ... the HELIO-HOPPER. It was made of three big ceiling fans—one on top to work as helicopter blades, and the other two on opposite sides to steer it. Below the fans were two side-by-side wheelchairs to sit in. And on the bottom of the chairs were plenty of springs (just in case the fans didn't work so well).

Cody's frown deepened as he said, "I'm just afraid Piper might be in trouble."

"Why's that?" Willard said as he returned to tightening the bolts on the helio-hopper.

"She said they took a bus to Pasadena."

Willard agreed. "That alone is an indication of something being incorrect."

Cody nodded. "Who would take a bus to visit their aunt all the way to Pasadena *without* their parents?"

Willard continued to tinker.

Cody nodded to the hopper. "I wish that thing was working so we could fly over there and check on her."

"You are in luck." He tightened the last bolt and looked up. "I believe we are ready for our first test flight."

"Cool!" Cody exclaimed. "Start her up."

Willard climbed aboard the helio-hopper and turned the key. It gave a grinding noise until the engine coughed to life.

"All right!" Cody shouted.

That was the good news. Unfortunately, there was also a little bad ...

The whole machine leaped suddenly into the air and crashed down onto the floor. Then it leaped higher and crashed harder.

"What's going on?" Cody yelled.

"It appears to be over-oscillating!"

"What does that mean?"

It shot up, nearly hitting the roof. "It means you better hurry and get on before we take off!"

Once again it slammed to the ground. This time Cody jumped into the empty chair just before it shot up and grazed the ceiling.

"Hang on!" Willard shouted as they crashed back down. "I suspect the next couple leaps will be the ones!"

"The ones for what?" Cody yelled.

Again they slammed into the ceiling. This time the

wooden planks gave a sickening *CRACK* before the helio-hopper fell back to the floor.

"The ones for what?" Cody repeated.

Again, they shot up, hitting the ceiling with such force that it finally gave way. The wood splintered into a thousand pieces as the boys and machine shot through the roof and up into the sky.

●

Piper stood at Aunt Myrna's doorway beside Zach and in front of Elijah. She couldn't put her finger on it, but something was stopping her from entering.

Maybe it was the forced smile on the woman's face—a smile that looked more painted than real.

Maybe it was the fact there were no cars parked out front—not Aunt Myrna's, not Dad's.

But she suspected the real reason was that Elijah had grabbed the back of her belt and held her, not letting her go inside the house.

"Please," the woman repeated. "I really think it's time to come in, don't you?"

"Oh, yes," Piper agreed. Once again she tried moving forward, and once again Elijah held her back.

Finally, she turned to him. "What is the matter with you?"

The little guy gave no answer but narrowed his eyes and pulled even harder.

Just then the phone rang from inside the house.

"Oh, that must be your parents now," the woman said.

Zach stepped inside. "Probably calling to see what we want on our pizza," he offered.

Piper looked at her little brother and decided she'd had enough. She reached back, grabbed Elijah by the hand, and pulled him inside with her. "Tell them I want extra sausage," she said.

"Yes." The woman smiled painfully as she shut the door. "Extra sausage."

●

By now, Willard and Cody were fifty feet in the air—dipping and diving, spinning and twirling—all the time hanging on for dear life.

Cody yelled, "Can't you—*WOAHH, WHAAA, WOOO*—steer this thing?!"

"Of course!" Willard shouted back. "Just as soon as I get a little—*WOOO, WHAAA, WOAHH*—practice!"

And practice he did as they dove this way and that, then that way and this . . . barely missing trees, telephone wires, and more than one angry seagull.

After twenty or thirty minutes of these fun and games, Willard finally started getting the hang of it.

"Isn't this cool?" he shouted.

Cody would have been happy to answer, but he was too busy hanging his head over the side of his chair, trying not to throw up. When he finally looked over to Willard, he saw his friend managing the controls with one hand while at the same time pressing buttons on a small box.

"What's that?" Cody yelled.

"My GPS tracker!" Willard shouted.

"Your what?"

"I believe there is a way we can find Piper's location!"

"How?"

"With a few modifications to this device, it is possible to locate her cell phone signal and trace it."

"Great!" Cody shouted. "That's just—" He wanted to finish the sentence, but it was more important he throw his head back over the side and hope there was nobody standing directly below him when he barfed.

Zach, Piper, and Elijah stood in the living room as the woman answered the phone.

"Hello, Mike? Good. The kids are here." She looked at them and tried another smile. "Yes, they seem fine."

Piper felt a wave of relief and smiled back.

The woman continued talking. "Yes, I'll tell them. Oh, and remember your daughter likes extra sausage on her pizza. Yes, we'll see you soon."

At last she hung up. "They'll be here in a little while."

"Great," Zach said as he plopped down on the sofa.

Feeling better, Piper joined him. Only Elijah remained standing. "C'mon, Eli." Piper held out her hands. "Come sit with me."

But Elijah refused. Instead, he turned and walked back to the front door.

The woman tensed. "He's not leaving, is he?"

"Nah," Zach assured her. "He'll stay with us."

The woman continued to watch.

"You'll have to excuse him," Piper explained. "Sometimes he acts a little ... strange."

"Yes." The woman nodded, not taking her eyes from Elijah. "So I've heard."

"Hey, pal," Zach called. "What are you—"

Elijah reached up and locked the front door with a loud *CLICK*.

Piper shrugged. "Guess he's afraid of burglars."

"Yes." The woman nodded again. "That must be it."

Suddenly the door knob rattled. Someone was trying to get in.

Zach rose from the sofa to take a peak out the window. Concerned, Piper joined him.

"It's probably just those annoying Girl Scouts," the woman said. "They're always trying to sell those awful cookies."

But they were not Girl Scouts. Instead, one was a big hulk of a man with a funny face. The other was the skinny guy with the long, pointed nose that Piper had seen pulling out a gun in front of her house—the very same gun he was pulling out now!

Without a word, Piper spun around and headed for the kitchen.

The woman turned. "Is everything . . . all right?"

"Oh, yes." Piper fought to keep her voice even. "I was just wondering—" She silently motioned for Zach to follow. This time, for whatever reason, he decided to listen. So did Elijah. "*We* were just wondering if there was anything we could snack on while we waited?"

The woman looked unsure whether to follow them or unlock the door. She voted for the door. And that was all the time they needed.

Piper raced for the back kitchen door and threw it open. Her brothers followed right behind.

They leaped off the porch and dashed to the toolshed their dad had helped build a couple summers back.

Zach tugged at the shed's door. "Locked!" he whispered.

They turned, searching the yard. Elijah pointed at the old RV beside the house some twenty feet away. Zach nodded. "It's worth a try."

They ran to it and barely arrived on the other side when the porch light flooded the yard. "They're out here!" the woman shouted.

"I knew she was up to something," Piper whispered as she tried the RV door. It wouldn't budge.

"Try jiggling the handle," Zach said. "Maybe it's stuck." Piper tried again with no luck.

They heard footsteps coming down the porch stairs.

"What'll we do?" Piper whispered. She spotted Elijah feeling under the front bumper. "Elijah!"

The voices began to approach.

"Look in that shed," the woman ordered. "I'll check the RV."

"Elijah, what are you —"

Suddenly her little brother held up the hide-a-key he'd found under the front bumper. Zach quickly grabbed it and unlocked the door. "Everyone inside," he whispered.

They didn't have to be asked twice.

When they were all in, Zach locked the door behind them. "Crouch down so they can't see," he whispered.

The voices drew closer.

Zach reached over and silently pulled Elijah out of the light streaming in through the RV's windshield ... just as the door rattled.

Piper caught her breath.

"It's locked," the woman called. "Shine your light inside."

A flashlight beam blazed through the windshield. Piper pressed flat against the wall. So did Zach and Elijah. They watched, frozen, as the beam moved across the floor and walls.

Another light appeared through the side window. Piper prayed silently as it crept toward them. They were going to be spotted any second.

Zach motioned them under the kitchen table. Piper

nodded. It was their only hope. Silently, Zach and Eli darted under it without a problem.

But Piper was a fraction too slow. The beam caught her arm and she froze. It passed her, hesitated, and then darted back.

# Chapter Five

## Hide-and-Go-EEK!

On its next pass through the RV, the beam caught the edge of Piper's arm just as Zach grabbed her and dragged her under the table.

The light continued to shoot back, then forward, then back again, just inches from them. But it found nothing.

All while this happened, the red-haired woman continued yanking and pulling at the door.

Piper prayed quietly. She threw a glance to Zach and noticed he was doing the same. But not Elijah. Instead, the little guy was sitting there actually grinning. Weird.

The shaking of the door handle stopped.

"They musta gone down the alley," a man's voice said.

"Check it out," the woman ordered. "Bruno, go the other way."

"What are you going to do?" the other voice asked.

"Call the Compound. Now hurry! We've got to find them!"

The beams of light disappeared, and the footsteps began moving off.

●

Willard zipped over houses, roads, and a freeway or two. The good news was Cody had nothing left to throw up. The bad news was he was still sicker than a dog.

Willard's flying had improved quite a bit. And, other than that one close call with the 747 coming in for a landing (never fly a helio-hopper near a major airport) he did pretty well. Soon, they were soaring over the homes in Pasadena.

"We're getting close!" he shouted, looking at the GPS tracker. "She's in this neighborhood."

"I hope she's okay," Cody yelled back. "There was something about her voice."

Moment's later, Willard shouted, "I'm landing! The last transmission was on this block!"

Cody nodded as Willard reduced power. Unfortunately, he reduced it just a little too much and they fell like a rock.

"AUGH!" Cody yelled.

"AUGH!" Willard agreed.

They slammed hard onto the road and—*BOING!*—bounced back up. And slammed hard and—*BOING!* And slammed hard and—Well, you get the picture. Finally, after a couple minutes of the pogo-stick imitation, they came to a stop.

"Well," Willard said as Cody threw up again, just for

old time's sake, "that was rather exciting." He turned to Cody and said, "You appear somewhat pale, my friend. Might I suggest you get a bit more sun?"

Cody said nothing. He was just grateful to be back on the ground. When he finally did speak, he managed to squeak out the words, "Are you sure this is the right place?"

"I'm double-checking," Willard said as he pressed more buttons on his GPS. "I'm triangulating the signal at this present time and ..." He hesitated.

"And what?" Cody asked.

Willard scowled hard at the numbers. "The call was transmitted within five feet of this very location."

Cody glanced around. "So where did they go?"

"Perhaps one of these houses is their aunt's residence."

"Yeah, but which one?"

"Why don't you call her and ask?" Willard said.

"Because ..." Cody came to a stop. "Because ..."

"What?" Willard asked.

"Why didn't we just call in the first place?"

Willard looked at him and shrugged. "An excellent observation, and one we should consider the next time we encounter a similar situation."

"You mean when we're not hanging on for our lives, trying not to die?" Cody said.

"Yes, something to that effect."

Cody shook his head and reached for his phone to dial Piper's number.

●

Inside the RV, Piper held her breath as the voices continued to fade.

Suddenly, her cell phone began playing, "If I Only Had a Brain."

"Shut it off!" Zach whispered.

She fumbled in her pocket and pulled out the phone. It nearly slipped from her hands as she struggled to turn it off.

●

Silas came to a stop at the porch steps. "Did you hear that?"

"Hear what?" Bruno asked.

"It was like music." He listened again. "It's gone now."

Up on the porch, Monica was pacing. There was nothing she hated worse than calling Shadow Man—especially when it came to giving him bad news.

The two men watched as her left eye began twitching the way it did whenever she became nervous.

"She's pretty upset," Silas whispered.

"Really?" Bruno replied. "Her foot ain't tapping."

"Not yet, but—"

Suddenly, her right foot began to tap.

"There it goes," Bruno whispered.

Silas nodded.

Both men looked on—Silas, because he was nervous; Bruno, because he was in love. Of course, Silas had tried to warn Bruno that it wasn't such a good idea falling in love with your boss. But whenever she was around, all fourteen or fifteen of Bruno's brain cells went into *hyper ga-ga*.

The third phase of Monica's nerves kicked in. She began swallowing ... hard.

*Twitch, twitch, tap, tap, swallow, swallow.*

*Swallow, swallow, tap, tap, twitch, twitch.*

"She's sooo beautiful," Bruno said with a sigh.

"Not now, you dork," Silas warned.

At last she reached for her phone and hit the speed dial.

●

In the dark mountain compound, the phone rang. A long shadowy arm reached for the receiver. "Yesss?" a voice hissed.

Monica answered, "We're still looking for them, sir."

A strange, screeching sound escaped from Shadow Man's throat. Then, after taking a deep breath, he asked, "Did they not come to the houssse?"

"Yes … they came in the front door and went out the back."

"You let them get away?"

"No, I mean, yes. I mean, we're looking for them right now and—"

Another screech leapt from Shadow Man's throat. Then, with a wheezing breath, he shouted, "You know what will happen if you fail!"

"Yes, sir."

"Then fiiiind themmm!!"

●

The kids huddled beneath the table in the dark. They could hear the woman shouting instructions. It sounded like she was leaving, but they couldn't be certain.

Always the "mom" of the group, Piper turned to see how Elijah was doing. But when she spotted him, he was grinning even bigger than before.

She glanced at Zach, who also saw it.

Then, ever so softly, Elijah began to hum.

Zach and Piper exchanged worried looks.

The humming grew louder until, very softly, Elijah began to sing. A hymn! Like they sang in church!

"Shh!" Zach warned. "Quiet, Elijah."

The boy opened his eyes. It almost looked like he was about to say something when, all of a sudden, someone banged on the door.

Zach and Piper froze. Elijah quit singing.

Someone banged on the door again.

"Maybe they'll go away," Piper whispered.

Elijah slipped out from under the table.

"Elijah!" Zach whispered.

But he didn't listen. Instead, he started for the door.

"Eli, get back here!"

Elijah reached for the handle and unlocked it.

Zach sprang toward him. But instead of stopping the boy, he tripped and slammed into him. The two fell into the door, which flew open. Unable to catch themselves, they tumbled out of the RV and onto the ground right in front of ... Cody and Willard!

Zach looked up at them in surprise. "What are you guys—"

"Shh!" Cody whispered. "They're searching the neighborhood for you."

Piper watched wide-eyed as the boys climbed back into the RV silently and shut the door.

"What are you doing here?" she whispered.

"I thought you were in some kind of trouble," Cody said, his blue eyes shining even in the dark.

Piper opened her mouth, but no words would come.

Willard explained. "We flew my helio-hopper over."

Before Piper could ask what a helio-whatever was, her brother had moved to the windshield and was looking outside.

"What do you observe?" Willard asked.

"They must have gone around front. They're nowhere in sight ... at least for now."

"What do we do?" Piper asked, still unable to take her eyes from Cody's.

Zach sighed heavily. "We can't stay here."

"Maybe we should make a run for it," Cody offered.

"I do not believe that is advisable," Willard said.

Piper nodded. "Willard's right. We can never outrun them ... at least not on foot."

As Cody's looked at the driver's seat, a thought began taking shape. "Who said anything about using our feet?" He moved to join Zach at the front of the RV. "Does this thing run?"

Zach looked to him, then back to the driver's seat. "I guess there's only one way to find out." He fished into his pocket to pull out the key Elijah had given him.

Piper's heart raced. "Zach, you're not going to try and start it?"

"You got any better ideas?"

Once again she opened her mouth, and once again there were no words.

Zach slipped into the seat, bent over to find the ignition, and inserted the key. "Well, here goes nothing."

And "nothing" is exactly what happened—except for the dull click of the starter.

He tried again.

Another click.

"Battery's dead," Cody said.

Zach nodded.

"Now what?" Piper groaned. She glanced back to Cody, who'd already turned to Willard.

"Well ..." Willard cleared his throat. "It is perhaps possible to connect the battery of my helio-hopper to the battery of the RV. That may generate enough electrical power to—"

"Right," Cody interrupted. "But we need jumper cables."

"There might be some in the shed," Zach suggested.

"It's locked," Piper reminded him.

"Perhaps we could reroute the starter to my battery," Willard suggested, "then onto the RV's battery — provided we can secure enough wire from the accessories panel."

The group traded looks.

"What are we waiting for?" Zach blurted. "Let's get to work!"

●

Mom and Dad had no idea where they were — it was some sort of storeroom with office supplies. They were tied together, back to back, in two wooden chairs. And, even though their backs were to each other, Dad could still hear his wife's quiet tears.

"Sweetheart, we've got to be strong," he said.

"I know," she answered hoarsely. "I just can't stop worrying about the kids."

"They'll be all right. Zach is tough. And Piper is smart."

She softly sniffed. "I just wish we could contact them. Let them know we're okay."

"And make sure they don't come looking for us," Dad added.

"Oh, Mike." She sucked in her breath. "You don't think they would, do you?"

To be honest, he wasn't certain. He wished he could warn them and tell them not to fall for any tricks. To help calm his wife, he tried changing the subject. "Let's see if we can get out of these ropes."

"How? They've got us tied so tightly I can barely move. No way can we break free of these chairs."

For the hundredth time, he tried moving his own arms and legs, and for the hundredth time he failed. She was absolutely right. There was nothing they could do. Unless ... An idea began to form. "Maybe we can't break free of the chairs," he said, "but ... maybe they can break free of us."

"What?"

"We can't move in these chairs. But if we could break one, it might give us room to wiggle. Here, start rocking with me."

"What do you—"

"The floor is concrete. If we fall over hard enough and slam the chairs into the concrete, we might be able to break them."

"Or our backs."

"It's worth a try," he said. "What else can we do?"

Mom had no answer.

He started to rock slowly. "Come on, join me."

She hesitated, and then finally began to rock with him.

"That's it," he said.

They rocked harder.

"Keep it up. And when we fall, smash as hard as you can onto the floor."

"Right."

Seconds later, it happened. The chairs tipped to the left. The couple leaned as hard as they could until they crashed onto the floor near the wall.

There was a loud CRACK.

"Did you hear that?" he asked.

"Yes."

"It was the arm. It's loose. Now if I can just wiggle my hand free."

Another moment and he shouted, "Got it!" With

his loose hand, he moved the ropes until he freed his other. Next he worked on his feet.

"Mike?" his wife asked in concern.

"Hang on, sweetheart, I'm just about there."

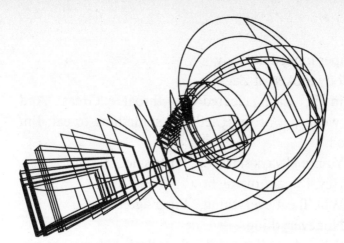

# Chapter Six

## The Escape

The RV was a mess. The protective cover between the front seats was off. The engine was exposed. And there were so many wires it looked like a spaghetti factory had exploded.

"How's it coming?" Piper asked, holding their one and only flashlight.

Cody looked up and gave her that killer smile of his. "Well, I think we've done as much damage as we can."

"Actually," Willard cleared his throat, "we have stripped the wires from the accessories panel in the RV and are quite certain it will carry the low voltage emitting from my helio-hopper battery. Then, of course, we must splice it back from the RV's starter into the RV's battery to maintain engine performance."

Piper looked at Cody.

Cody looked at Zach.

Finally, Zach cleared his throat. "Great. And once we're out of here, let's get something to eat. I'm starved."

"You're always starved," Piper said.

"Hey, I'm a growing boy."

"Who'll eat everything," Piper agreed.

"Not everything."

"What do you mean?'" she asked. "Name me one thing you won't eat."

"Remember the macaroni and cheese you tried frying up in mustard and ketchup?"

"Zach . . ."

"And covered in horseradish?"

Piper felt her ears growing hot. "It was an experiment."

"Tell that to Molly."

"Who's Molly?" Willard asked.

"Our dog," Zach explained. "Nobody would eat it so we gave it to her."

"What happened?"

"We had to take her to the vet."

"Zach . . ." Piper repeated her warning.

But her brother was on a roll and there was no stopping him. "To the emergency room—"

"Zach, please . . ." She stole a look over to Cody.

"Where they had to pump her stomach so she wouldn't die!" Zach broke out laughing. He could really crack himself up at times.

Piper would have joined in if she wasn't busy giving him one of her death ray stares . . . until she spotted Cody looking at her . . . until she suddenly changed it to a smile, trying to look all pleasant and polite.

Unfortunately, the look on Cody's face said she failed on both accounts.

After a lengthy pause that redefined the term *awkward*, Willard said, "I have half a burger and some fries left over in my sweatshirt pocket."

"Left over from what?" Zach asked.

"Lunch."

The group exchanged glances.

Willard reached into his pocket and explained, "Waste not, want not."

He pulled out the bag and handed it to Elijah, who sat the closest. But instead of passing the bag over, Elijah held it a moment. In the dim light it almost looked like he was moving his lips.

Paying no attention, Zach grabbed the bag from him and opened it. "I don't care what you got, I could eat a—" He came to a stop.

Cody looked over to him. "You okay?"

Zach stared into the bag but said nothing.

"Yo, Zach."

Finally, Zach spoke. "I thought you said there was only half a burger here."

Before Willard could answer, Zach pulled out an entire hamburger. Then he reached in and pulled out another. And another.

For the first time in his life, Zach was speechless.

Piper reached across the aisle and grabbed the bag. She stuck her hand inside ... and pulled out another!

"I don't get it," Willard said. "Where did I get those?"

Without a word, Piper passed the bag to Cody.

Cody took it and pulled out one, two, three bags of French fries.

No one said a word.

Piper nervously coughed. Finally she cleared her throat and asked, "So ... anybody want to say grace?"

●

Dad had wiggled out of the ropes and was helping Mom get free.

"There we go," he said as he pulled her last rope away. He reached to her arm and gently helped her to her feet. "You okay?"

She nodded, rubbing her wrists. "You?"

"Yeah." He moved across the room quickly and tried the door.

Locked.

No surprise there.

"Now what?" Mom asked.

He looked to the ceiling, to the walls, searching for any type of opening, any type of air duct.

Nothing.

Mom had moved to a shelf of stationery supplies. "Maybe there's something here."

He turned to her. "Like what?"

"I don't know. But we've got to do something."

Without another word, she reached for the nearest box and started to tear it open. Dad crossed the room and joined her.

●

Willard looked over the mass of wires and duct tape that led from the helio-hopper battery on the RV's kitchen table to the RV starter, and back to the RV's battery. "I believe we are ready for our first test."

"It better be a good one," Zach said as he pulled away from the window, "'cause they're headed back this way!" He turned to Piper and motioned for her to shut off the flashlight.

She nodded, but was too late.

Outside, the heavier male voice asked, "Did you see that?"

"A light in the RV!" the other man answered.

"Let's get 'em!" the first cried. Louder, he shouted, "We found 'em, Monica! They're in the RV!"

*Get down,* Zach motioned to everyone in the motor home. *Down.*

The door suddenly rattled. Zach had luckily had the good sense to lock it.

"A rock!" one of the men shouted. "Get that rock!"

There was a moment's silence. Then, a rock smashed the right door's window directly above Piper's head.

Piper gave a stifled scream and everyone stopped breathing.

The rock hit the window again ... and again, until finally the glass exploded.

Piper cried out as glass rained down all over her.

A hand reached inside, trying to unlock the door.

"What do we do?" Willard yelled.

"The only thing we can do!" Zach shouted. He jumped behind the wheel of the RV.

The hand had nearly found the lock. Without stopping to think, Piper pulled off her shoe and slammed the hand with it.

The man yelled in pain and the hand disappeared.

Zach tried the engine. There was a very faint whine, then nothing.

Everyone groaned.

The hand came back inside.

Piper hit it again, and again, as hard as she could.

But this time, it remained.

"It must work!" Willard exclaimed. "Everything is in place." Only then did he see Elijah pointing to a loose wire.

"Yes!" Willard lunged forward and reattached it.

Finally, the hand found the lock. Quickly, it unlocked the door.

Again, Zach turned the key. This time the engine sputtered to life ... just as the door flew open.

The big man reached inside. Piper was the closest, and he managed to grab hold of her sweatshirt. She screamed, trying to break away, but it did little good.

He had her.

Cody leaped into action. He plowed into the man as hard as he could. The man gasped and lost hold of Piper as Zach dropped the RV into gear and hit the gas.

Tires spun, spitting mud and gravel. The RV drifted to the right until Zach fought the wheel and straightened it.

The man's arms and head were still inside as he ran, trying to keep up.

The side gate lay dead ahead.

Zach pushed the pedal to the floor.

Piper screamed as they crashed through the gate, stripping the man away, while driving right over what was left of Willard's helio-hopper.

They bounced onto the street as Cody shut the door.

Piper raced to the back and looked out the window. She saw the two men and the woman racing for their green van.

"They're coming after us!" she yelled.

"Let 'em," Zach shouted as he looked in the rearview mirror. "No way will they catch us!"

# Chapter Seven

## The Hospital

Zach swerved crazily down the city street.

"Watch out!" Piper shouted as he barely missed his fourth (or was it fifth) parked car.

"This thing drives like a house!" Zach complained.

"You don't even have your license!" Piper cried.

"Details, details."

"You barely know how to drive!"

"Relax," he said with a grin. "It's just like a video game."

"Video games give you three crashes for a dollar!"

Zach turned to her. "How much money we got?"

"Stop joking!"

Zach continued to laugh. He could be so clever sometimes. At least he thought he could.

"Look out!" Piper cried as they drifted into the wrong lane. (Normally this wouldn't be a problem, except for the cement truck heading straight for them.)

"Zach!"

He turned just in time and yanked the wheel hard to the right so they barely missed crashing into it.

The mailbox on the other side of the road wasn't so lucky. Nor was the rosebush, or the pink plastic flamingos arranged on the front lawn. Well, they had been on the front lawn. Now they were crunching under the RV's tires, flying over the RV's roof, or hitching a free ride on the RV's bumper.

Once the fun and games were over, they bounced back onto the street and continued their little suicide ride.

"Excuse me," Willard interrupted, holding up his handheld computer. "If my calculations are correct, they will be catching up with us in roughly one minute and thirty-two seconds."

"Willard's right," Cody agreed. "There's no way we can outrun them in this thing."

"So what do we do?" Piper asked.

Willard answered. "Since the RV is so visible, I suggest we hide it."

"But where?"

Suddenly, Zach threw the RV into a hard left, tossing everyone to the side.

"Zach, what are you—" Then Piper saw it. He'd found an underground parking lot and was racing inside.

"They'll never find us here," he shouted.

"Uh, excuse me, Zach?" Willard called. "What is the maximum clearance of this structure and what is our vehicle's height?"

"Huh?"

Before he could repeat himself, the RV gave a sickening shudder as its plastic sky light was sheered off by one of the low-hanging concrete beams in the garage ceiling.

Zach hit the brakes and threw them all forward to the floor.

"Oh no!" Piper groaned. She staggered back to her feet. "Did you just do what I think you did?"

"Perhaps we should ascertain the damages," Willard suggested.

"Yeah," Zach agreed. "Perhaps we should."

As they stepped from the RV, Piper spotted a sign that read *Eastwood Hospital Parking*.

"Well, at least we know where we are," she said.

They boosted Zach up to the top of the RV to see what had happened.

"Doesn't look too bad," he called over his shoulder. "Where did all these pieces of flamingos come from?"

"What about the RV?" Piper asked. "Is the RV okay?"

"The roof might leak a bit, but we could stuff a blanket in to stop that."

Willard and Cody helped Zach back down as Piper asked, "So what's our plan now?"

"Go to the police?" Cody offered.

Zach shook his head. "Kids against adults—who do you think they'd believe?"

Piper nodded. "Especially when one of those kids has just stolen an RV, illegally driven it, and crashed it into a parking-garage ceiling."

"Hey," Cody asked, "where's your little brother?"

Piper glanced around. He was nowhere in sight.

"Eli?" Zach stuck his head into the RV. "Little buddy, you in here?"

Nothing.

"Where could he have gone?" Piper asked. She tried unsuccessfully to keep the fear out of her voice. "You don't think that they, they—"

"We'd have seen them, Pipe," Zach said. "Nobody grabbed him. But why would he just slip off?"

Piper glanced up at the Eastwood Hospital Parking sign. "Wait a minute."

"What?" Cody asked.

"Earlier today," she turned to Zach, "remember he wanted to go visit a hospital?"

"So?" Zach asked.

"So maybe he's doing that now."

Zach began to nod slowly.

"But why?" she asked.

"Why does he do half the things he does?" Zach said.

Piper shrugged. He had a point.

"Perhaps we should commence searching for him?" Willard offered.

No one disagreed. But nobody suggested how to begin either.

Finally, Cody spoke up. "Why don't Willard and I check out everywhere on this block."

Zach nodded. "I'll check the block across the street and behind us."

Cody continued. "And Piper, why don't you look in the hospital?"

"But what if . . ." Piper's voice was suddenly clogged with emotion. "What if we can't find him?" She looked down, letting her hair drop over her face.

Cody waited until she looked back up. Then, holding her eyes, he said softly, "We'll find him, Piper. Don't worry. We'll find him."

"But what if—" Her voice cracked and she couldn't continue.

Ever so gently, he put an arm around her. Then he turned to the group. "Let's all meet back here in one hour. If we don't find him by then ..." He hesitated. "Then we'll call the police."

●

Five minutes later, Piper arrived at the Information Desk in the hospital lobby. A silver-haired woman was frantically answering phones while pointing out directions to various visitors.

"Excuse me?" Piper asked. "Excuse me?"

A third phone rang. The woman motioned for Piper to wait as she answered it.

Piper blew the hair out her eyes and glanced around the lobby. The place was huge, and modern art covered the walls. In the middle of the room stood the world's ugliest statue. She couldn't figure out if it was supposed to be a spiderweb, a boney hand, or some stringy alien spacecraft visiting from another planet.

It made no difference. Piper was not crazy about visiting hospitals. Actually, it wasn't the hospitals, it was the people suffering in them. She'd never forget the time she volunteered as a candy striper. On her first day of the job, a nurse asked her to help change the dressing on an old man's wound.

It wasn't too bad—just a deep gash along his belly where a piece of metal had dug in from a car crash. And Piper didn't have to do any of the work. All she had to do was hold the bandages as the nurse unwound them.

No problem.

The problem came when they peeled back the old bandages and Piper saw the open wound. Actually, it wasn't the "seeing" that was the problem ... it was the getting sick to her stomach, the feeling her face break out in a sweat, and the fainting right there onto the floor that was a bit embarrassing.

When she woke up, the nurse was helping her to her feet.

"Sweetheart, are you okay?" she'd asked.

Of course, Piper had pretended nothing was wrong, that she'd tripped or stumbled or something. And she might have pulled it off ...

Except for the part of seeing the open wound again, breaking out in a sweat again, and, you guessed it, hitting the floor again.

So much for her career in the medical field.

"May I help you?"

The voice drew her out of her memories and back into the lobby. She looked at the silver- haired lady and cleared her throat. "Did you see a little boy come in here? Six years old, dark hair, and glasses that are—"

"Is he lost?"

"Well, no. I mean, maybe. I don't know."

The woman's smile froze slightly.

Realizing how lame she sounded, Piper tried again. "Actually, I'm not even sure he's here."

The frozen smile cracked slightly.

Luckily, another phone rang. The woman reached for it and answered it. "Good afternoon, Eastwood Hospital. How may I help you?" Then another rang. "Would you hold, please? Good afternoon, Eastwood Hospital. How may I help you?"

Piper glanced around. It was pretty obvious that the only way she could find Elijah was to look for him herself. With a sigh, she turned from the desk and started for the elevators. But she'd only taken a few steps before she heard, "Miss ... Miss."

She turned to see the woman at the desk calling to

her. "I'm sorry, but children are not allowed to visit without an adult."

"Child? I'm no child. I'm almost—"

"Sorry, those are the rules." The phone rang again, and she answered it. "Good afternoon, Eastwood Hospital, how may I help you?"

Across the lobby, the doors to the elevator opened. For a second, Piper thought of racing onto it—rules or no rules. But knowing the woman was keeping an eye on her, and that she had broken more than the daily minimum requirement of rules for one day, Piper turned and slowly started for the exit.

With each step she took, her heart grew heavier. Things were finally catching up with her—leaving the house, losing Mom and Dad, and now ... her baby brother. Why was everything so hard? What was the big secret her parents kept hiding from her? And why, just when things started to get normal, did stuff like this always happen?

She stepped out the hospital doors and into the sunlight. Tears filled her eyes. She blinked them back. She would not cry. Not now. Not when Elijah needed her. She swallowed hard, then thought back to the Bible verse Mom and Dad had left them: "I am with you always."

It sure didn't feel like anybody was with her. It felt more like she was lost and alone. Very, very alone.

"Where are you, God?" she whispered to herself. "Where are—"

"Excuse me?"

She turned and saw an old man holding his chest, leaning against the building.

"I think ... I'm ... having a heart attack," he said.

Piper rushed to his side.

"Hospital," he gasped. "I must get to—"

"It's here!" she said. She searched the building. "You just passed the emergency exit. It's back there!"

The man turned, but could barely stand.

"C'mon." She slipped her shoulder under his arm. "I'll help you!"

"Thank ..." He could say no more.

They headed down the sidewalk as fast as they could. But even as Piper helped the man, she sensed there was something familiar about him. She'd seen him somewhere. They were a dozen feet from the hospital doors when she heard Zach shouting across the street.

"Piper? What's up?"

She turned as he ran to join them. "This man, he's having a heart attack," she shouted.

Zach arrived and moved to the man's other side.

"Thank you," the man gasped. "Thank you."

Zach nodded. Glancing to Piper, he asked, "Any sign of Eli?"

Piper shook her head no. "You?"

"Nothing."

They reached the emergency entrance. The doors hissed open, and within seconds an orderly was at their side. Grabbing a wheelchair, he eased the man down as a nurse arrived with a clipboard.

"What's your name, sir?" she asked.

"Gabriel," he wheezed.

"Like the angel?"

He nodded.

The nurse wrote it down and turned to the orderly. "Let's get Mr. Gabriel inside, stat."

They rolled him toward a pair of frosted-glass doors. But when the doors slid opened, Piper caught her breath. For there, just inside the hallway, stood her little brother.

"Elijah!" She called.

The boy looked up and smiled.

Zach saw him too.

But when they started toward him, Elijah turned and raced down the hall.

"Elijah!" Zach called. "Eli!"

By the time they got inside the door, their little brother was nowhere to be found.

●

Monica, Silas, and Bruno cruised the streets in their van.

"How could a huge motor home just vanish?" Monica demanded.

"Well ... uh ... maybe we can't see it," Bruno offered.

"I know we can't see it," Monica snapped. "Otherwise we'd ... *see* it."

"Uh, yeah." Bruno gave a giggle. "That's what I thought too."

Monica looked at him, thought of saying something, then figured it would do no good.

"Maybe they're hiding it," Silas suggested.

"Where do you hide a motor home?" Monica grunted.

Silas immediately hit the brakes, and they all flew forward.

"What are you doing?!" Monica demanded.

He said nothing but pointed to the building directly beside them—the one with the sign reading *Underground Parking*.

"Yes!" she exclaimed. "Yes! They could have hidden it in a parking garage. Let's check them all out. There can't be that many. Let's search every parking garage until we find them!"

Mom and Dad continued rummaging through the storage room, tearing through box after box of stationery supplies.

"These people must sure like notes," Mom said as she tossed another box of sticky notes to the side.

Dad nodded and glanced to the door. "What we really need is something to help us pop that lock. If they hadn't taken my wallet, I could have used a credit card or at least a—" He stopped, seeing a look of hope cross Mom's face.

"What about a metal ruler?" she asked. "I've got a whole box of them right here."

"Let's see one."

She handed him a ruler and he headed for the door.

Mom followed as he crouched down to peer through the small crack between the door and the frame. Then, ever so carefully, he slipped the ruler into the crack and tried to catch the underside of the bolt.

A moment later the door gave a click.

"Got it!" he said.

"Now what?"

"Now we try to find a way out of here."

●

The children's surgical unit was on the fourth floor of the hospital. There, in a small conference room, an older doctor spoke to some very frightened parents.

"We feel that brain surgery is the only chance for LeAnne's survival. But, at best, it's only a fifty-fifty chance."

A long pause followed before the father cleared his throat. "Those aren't great odds, Doctor."

The doctor nodded. "I understand how you feel. But, as you know, we have the best surgeons in the city for this kind of procedure."

The father nodded. "That's why we had her transferred here. But only fifty-fifty ..."

Another pause followed.

Finally the doctor answered. "A fifty-fifty chance is better than no chance. And that's what she'll have if we don't operate."

Across from the room an elevator dinged. The father looked into the hall to see the elevator's door open and a six-year-old boy with dark hair and glasses appear. The boy stepped into the hallway, looked both directions, and then headed for the children's ICU.

●

The green van entered the hospital's parking garage.

"There it is!" Silas shouted.

After three garages, they'd finally found the right one.

Silas brought the van to a stop and stepped out. Pulling his gun from his waistband, he silently approached the RV. He opened the door carefully and looked inside. No one was in sight.

"It's empty!" he called back to Monica.

Monica nodded. "All right then. Let's you and I comb the area. Bruno, you stay here in case they come back."

Bruno replied. "Yes, dear Monica. Your wish is my command."

Monica gave him a look, then shouted, "Knock it off!"

# Chapter Eight

## The Noose Tightens

Elijah peered around the corner into the ICU.

There were a dozen beds with all sorts of hanging bottles that were dripping and electronic gadgets that were beeping. At the far end, two nurses were speaking to a young doctor. But it was the third bed that caught Elijah's attention.

The girl he'd seen hit by the car was lying in it.

She looked awful. There were tubes running into her nose, mouth, and arms. Her skin was as pale as paper.

Slowly, Elijah made his way toward her. But he didn't get far.

"You there," a bald orderly called out from behind him. "Little boy."

Elijah froze a moment and then continued forward.

The voice continued. "You're not supposed to be in here."

Elijah was only a few steps from the bed when the orderly's huge hands grabbed him by the collar.

Within seconds, he was back outside the ICU with the orderly waving his finger in his face. "Children are not allowed in there. Where are your parents?"

Elijah shrugged.

The orderly grabbed him by the arm and escorted him down the hall to the reception desk. Here he spoke to an angry-looking nurse. "I caught this kid in ICU. Do you know who he belongs to?"

The nurse shook her head and eyed Elijah suspiciously. "How'd you get up here?"

Elijah turned and pointed at the elevator.

"I see," the nurse said. "He probably just wandered on and pushed a button. Call Security. They'll find his parents."

The orderly nodded. He pointed to a chair next to the desk. "Sit there!" he ordered as he reached for the phone. "We'll find your parents."

Elijah sat with a quiet sigh. He only wished that the man was right.

●

Dad looked around the corner and down the hall toward the exit.

Two burly guards stood at the front door. They didn't wear uniforms. In fact they looked more like thugs than security guards. Both wore shoulder holsters with guns.

"Someone's coming," Mom whispered from behind him.

Dad pulled back, took her hand, and together they darted to the nearby stairwell. "Upstairs," he whispered.

They stole up the steps silently until they reached the second level, where Dad checked out the hall, making sure the coast was clear.

"C'mon," he said.

They stepped into the hallway and moved past a bunch of offices. The first two were lit and had people talking inside. The third was dark. He reached for the knob and gave it a try.

It opened with a quiet creak, and they stepped inside.

The office was small with only a desk, metal filing cabinet, phone, and computer. There were no windows.

Spotting the phone, Mom reached for it, but Dad stopped her. He pointed to the blinking lights on it. "Someone will see the light. Let's try the computer instead."

Mom nodded as Dad sat down in front of the computer and worked the keys. She began to pray quietly.

Moment's later the email screen popped up.

"Yeah, baby!" Dad whispered. Then turning to Mom he asked, "So what do we say?"

"Write the kids first," she whispered. "Tell them we're okay. *And* tell them not to try and find us."

Dad started typing. "Got it."

"And after that ..." Mom took a breath. "After that, have them call the police."

●

In the dark room, Shadow Man stared at the photo of Elijah Dawkins. He drummed his fingers on his jet-black desk. "So young," he muttered. "And already such a threat."

Just then, a tiny green light on the signal board next to his computer lit up. Frowning, he picked up the phone and pressed a key.

"Who isss usssing the sssystem in room 211?" he demanded.

"I don't know, sir," came the reply.

"Find out and report to me at onccce. There should be no one in that officcce."

"Yes, sir."

Shadow Man stared at the green light a moment, his suspicions growing.

"Is there anything else, sir?"

"Yesss. Kill the computer line in Room 211."

"The computer line, sir?"

"Yeesss! Shut it down, now!"

"Yes, sir."

Shadow Man slammed down the receiver and glared at the light. A moment later it went dark.

●

Elijah fidgeted in his seat.

The nurse gave him a nasty look.

He fidgeted again.

She looked at him again.

Finally, she picked up the phone, dialed, and spoke. "Hello, Security, have you found the boy's parents yet? He's driving me nuts." She listened a moment. "Well, keep looking. Oh, and send someone up here to take him off my hands. He can wait in *your* office."

She hung up the phone and glared at Elijah.

He fidgeted.

She glared some more.

Moments later, a gray-haired orderly arrived.

"That was fast," the nurse said. "Are you here for the kid?"

The orderly nodded.

"All he does is stare at me with those huge eyes of his and fidget. Stare and fidget. Stare and fidget. He's driving me crazy."

The old man nodded again and held out his hand. Elijah smiled, slipped out of his chair, and grabbed onto the man's hand.

They headed down the hall. But instead of going to the elevator, the orderly took him directly to ICU.

Elijah looked up at him and grinned wider. The old man smiled back.

Suddenly, the double doors opened, and a doctor and several nurses walked by. But for some strange reason they didn't even notice Elijah and the orderly. Then, from the opposite direction, a bald orderly also passed.

But, again, he didn't see either one of them.

The gray-haired orderly released Elijah's hand and nodded. Elijah returned the nod and entered ICU.

He approached the third bed, the one where the little girl slept. Then, ever so gently, he reached over and touched her head.

●

"Something's wrong," Dad said. "I've lost the signal."

Mom looked alarmed. "Did you get a message out?"

"I think so ... at least to the kids. But—"

The office door exploded open, and two big thugs entered.

"Don't move," the first ordered. "Don't touch the keyboard."

Dad nodded. "The signal's shut down anyway."

Finally, a third man came into the room—the strangest person Mom or Dad had ever seen.

He was huge, a good four hundred pounds. Somehow his head didn't quite match his body. But there was something even stranger. Even in the light, parts of the man could barely be seen. It was like he was constantly cloaked in shadow. It made no difference how directly the light shown on him; parts of his body, especially his face, could never be seen completely.

"Very clever, Mr. Dawkinsss." The man seemed to hiss more than speak. "I sssee you have sssent a messsage. "

Stepping closer to the computer, the man stared at what Dad had been writing.

Of course, Dad turned, trying to delete the message. The man made a horrible sound like a screaming, suffering animal. Dad was then thrown across the room as easily as if he were a rag doll.

He crashed into the filing cabinet and slid to the floor. Mom screamed and ran to him.

The man of shadows hunched over the computer. "Ssso. Sssending messagesss, are we? Perhapsss I can asssist you."

He stared hard at the computer. Then, to Mom and Dad's amazement, the keys suddenly began moving on their own.

The man read the words as they appeared on the screen:

DEAR KIDS,

DISREGARD PREVIOUS MESSAGE. NEED HELP.

BEING HELD AT COMPOUND IN MOUNTAINS. COME FOR US. MAKE SURE ELIJAH IS WITH YOU. DIRECTIONS ARE BELOW.

MOM AND DAD

The man turned to the couple and laughed at the look of alarm on their faces. "Don't worry. I'll give them very clear directionsss. They'll have no trouble finding usss."

"This is one big hospital!" Zach complained as he plopped down on the sofa in the third-floor waiting area.

"He's gotta be here," Piper said. "We both saw him."

"But where? And why is he hiding from us?"

Piper shook her head and glanced at her watch. "Oh, great, we were supposed to meet up with Cody and Willard four and a half minutes ago."

Zach snorted at her exactness.

"Well, we were," she insisted.

"Right."

"We should get them. See if they'll help us look."

Zach nodded and lumbered to his feet. "All right. I'll go. You keep looking." He started for the stairs.

"And tell them we're sorry for being late," she called.

Without turning, Zach gave a wave and continued toward the stairway.

●

Elijah slipped out of ICU and into the hall. He made his way quickly toward the elevator. Now he would find Piper and Zach. He pushed the call button, and moments later the elevator door opened. He checked the hall one last time as he backed inside.

"Can you believe this?" a man behind him said. "Right into our hands."

Elijah spun around to see the skinny man with the pointed nose ... and the woman with the bright red hair.

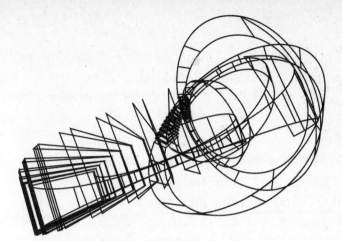

# Chapter Nine

## Race for Your Life

Zach spotted Cody standing next to the RV in the garage.

"Hey," he shouted. "Elijah's running around somewhere in the hospital. We need you guys to help us find him."

"Uh ..." Cody raised his eyebrows, blinked twice, and nodded his head to the right. "We can't, uh, come right now."

"Why not?" Zach asked as he approached. "And where's Willard?"

"He's, uh ..." Cody did the same weird eyebrow raising, blinking, and nodding. "We're working on the RV."

Zach frowned. "Why do you keep blinking like that?"

"I'm not blinking," Cody said as he blinked, raised his eyebrows, and nodded to the right.

"You're blinking right now. What's the matter with you?"

"I'm—

"What's the matter?" the big guy who had been chasing them said as he stepped out from behind the RV. In his hand he held a gun pointed at Cody.

"Why didn't you say something?" Zach asked Cody. "Or try to signal me? And what was with all the blinking and nodding?"

Cody shook his head in dismay. "That *was* me signaling you."

"Oh," Zach said, suddenly feeling anything but smart.

"So, uh, your brother's in the hospital, and your sister's looking for him?" the big man asked as he flipped open his cell phone.

"What?" Zach exclaimed. "Where'd you get that idea?"

Unfortunately, the only thing Zach was worse at than understanding blinking and nodding signals was his ability to act. And, even though the big guy wasn't the brightest candle on the cake, he saw through it in a second. He pushed a number on his cell phone. After a moment, he spoke into it.

"Yeah it's me, Bruno," he said. "The older brother came back. His sister's looking for the kid in the—What? You got him already? Great ... Yeah, we'll, uh, wait right here."

Zach and Cody exchanged nervous looks as the big man hung up and flashed them a menacing grin.

●

Piper had gone downstairs to the lobby to meet the others when she froze. There, coming off the elevator, was the woman with the bright red hair. Next to her was the skinny assistant. And between them, holding their hands, was . . .

"Elijah!" she gasped.

She ducked around the corner and watched from across the lobby. Desperately, she looked for a policeman, for any security.

There were none. Only—

She had another surprise. There, coming from the opposite direction, was the old man they had helped who had been having a heart attack. Only now he looked perfectly healthy!

He spotted her and gave a nod. But not a "hi-there, good to-see-you" nod. No, this was more like an insider's nod, the type that said, "You and I know something those others don't."

Piper stared at him, not understanding, as he continued walking . . . straight toward Elijah and the two grown-ups.

When he was ten feet from them, he suddenly broke out coughing—huge, violent coughs, like he was choking. He grabbed his throat as if he couldn't breathe.

The woman and man tried to sidestep him, but he suddenly reeled as if he was going to fall. And he did. Right into the woman with red hair.

She let out a yelp and lost her grip on Elijah as she and the old man tumbled to the ground. Her assistant tried to grab the boy, but the old man went into another coughing spasm and threw himself onto the assistant.

Suddenly, Piper understood. She darted around the corner and raced at them.

"Run, Elijah," she shouted. "Run!"

Her brother looked up and grinned as Piper arrived and grabbed his hand. But as they turned for the door, she spotted something. The woman's cell phone had spilled out of her purse and onto the floor.

In one quick move, Piper scooped it up, and they raced for the exit.

●

Back on the fourth floor, the little girl's parents stepped out of the conference room. They looked worn, tired, and very scared. Beside them was the doctor.

"I'll have the nurses begin prepping her for surgery right away," he said. "We'll begin in one hour."

The couple nodded sadly, and the husband did his best to support his wife.

Then, a young nurse from ICU rounded the corner.

"Nurse," the doctor said, "I want you to start prepping LeAnne Howard for surgery. We're going to—"

"But Doctor," she interrupted. "That's why I was coming to see you. LeAnne's awake. She's out of the coma!"

"What?" the doctor exclaimed.

"She seems to be fine. I know it's hard to believe, but there's absolutely nothing wrong with her!"

The doctor traded looks with the parents. Then, without a word, all four broke into a run toward the ICU.

●

Piper raced down the street toward the parking garage. She glanced over her shoulder, but neither the redhead nor her assistant had left the hospital yet. That old guy must really be keeping them busy.

Piper noticed the woman's cell phone had begun

to vibrate. She looked at it in her hand and hesitated. Should she answer it?

It vibrated again.

Approaching an alley, they ducked into it and she came to a stop.

The phone vibrated again.

She stared at it. Then, with a deep breath, she opened the lid and listened.

The voice on the other end paused a moment, then asked. "Monica?"

Piper fumbled with her shirt sleeve and brought it up to the phone. In a deep voice, she answered, "Yes?"

"I'm, uh, just checkin' in," he said. "You about here?"

Using her deepest voice, she answered, "Yeah, we're on our way."

"That's, uh, real good. 'Cause I got them other three all tied up nice and neat in the RV."

Piper's mind raced. They'd found the RV! They'd tied up Zach, Cody, and Willard! Now what? Where could she go, how could she help them, and what should she say?

Fortunately, the guy on the phone saved her the trouble.

"You, uh, want me to come pick you up?"

Piper's heart skipped. "Yes!" she cried. Then, remembering to lower her voice, she repeated, "Yes, leave the others, and pick us up in the van at the front of the hospital."

"Good, and then maybe we can buy you some cough drops."

Piper frowned. "Cough drops?"

"For your voice. It sounds like you're getting a cold."

"Uh, yes," Piper said, then gave a couple coughs for good measure. "Cough drops would be nice."

"Okay. Roger, ten–four, over and, uh ... uh ..."

"Out?" Piper suggested.

"Yeah." He giggled. "And out."

Piper pushed the End button and leaned against the wall with a huge sigh. Reaching down for Elijah's hand, she poked her head back out of the alley to check for the redhead, and then she turned and started for the parking garage.

Thirty seconds later, she arrived at the entrance only to hear a car racing down the ramp. She pulled Elijah out of sight just as the green van sped out and screeched a hard left toward the hospital.

As soon as the coast was clear, she raced into the garage and down the ramp where they'd parked the RV.

As she came closer she thought she heard muffled sounds from inside.

Once she arrived, she opened the door and, sure enough, there was Zach, Cody, and Willard all tied together with duct tape over their mouths.

"We've got to get out of here fast," she said as she and Elijah clambered inside.

"Hmmmph! Hummph!" Zach said.

"Hang on," Piper said as she kneeled down and tore off his duct tape.

"Ow!" Zach cried. "That hurt."

Grabbing a knife from the kitchen drawer, Piper quickly cut his ropes then removed Cody's tape — much more carefully.

"Thanks." Cody flashed her his grin.

Piper nodded.

Zach was already up and heading over to start the RV. "You guys hold on," he said. "Going up this ramp might be bumpy."

He fired up the RV, hit the gas, and they lurched forward.

"Zach!" Piper cried as she nearly fell.

But that was only the beginning. They hit the first speed bump and the RV's roof slammed hard into the ceiling, knocking the rest of the sky light off.

"*Zach!*" everyone shouted.

He slowed but paid no attention to the concrete beam hanging down in front of them ... until there was the sickening *SCREEECH! K-THUNK!* as the RV wedged itself underneath the beam and completely stopped.

"*ZACH*!"

He gunned it, but the RV wouldn't budge.

He threw it into reverse and revved the engine.

Repeat in the no-budge department.

●

Finally Monica and Silas broke free of the coughing old man and raced outside the hospital ... just in time to see Bruno pulling up in the van.

"What is he doing?!" Monica cried.

"Maybe he caught the kid," Silas said.

Monica threw him a look. Somehow she suspected that wasn't the case.

●

Back in the RV, Piper shouted, "What're we going to do? They'll be here any minute!"

"Let's all get out and push," Cody suggested.

It was as good an idea as any. Everyone but Zach piled out of the RV and lined up behind the rear bumper.

"Ready," Cody shouted. "One, two, three ... push!"

They pushed, and Zach revved the engine.

Nothing happened.

"Harder!" Zach called out the driver's window.

Again he revved, and again they pushed. But nothing seemed to work. They were stuck for good.

"Maybe we should run for it on foot!" Piper shouted.

"Five youngsters running on foot," Willard said. "I am afraid that will draw far too much attention."

"I'm open to other suggestions," Piper snapped.

Unfortunately, everybody seemed to have one ... all at the same time.

As the noise and shouting continued, Piper looked for Elijah. She spotted him kneeling at the front wheel.

"Eli!" she called. "What're you doing?"

The group came to a stop and looked.

"He's letting air out of the tire!" Cody said.

"Eli, stop that!" she shouted.

"No, no," Willard said. "That's a good thing. A little air out of each tire may lower the vehicle enough to allow the appropriate clearance."

The kids exchanged surprised looks ... and then each raced for a different tire.

●

"I didn't tell you to pick us up in front of the hospital!" Monica shouted.

"On the phone ... you, uh, said to hurry," Bruno argued. "You said you had the kid and—"

"You idiot! I don't even have my cell phone! How could—" Monica stopped in mid-sentence, suddenly realizing who *did* have her phone.

"Hurry!" she screamed. She threw open the van door and crawled inside. "Get back to the parking garage!"

Bruno frowned. "Does this mean we won't be getting you the cough drops?"

"*Hurry!*"

●

"That should do it," Zach called from the driver's window. "Now everyone get back inside!"

The group climbed back into the RV, and Cody had barely shut the door before Zach pressed his foot on the gas.

There was another crunching sound, but this time it was different—more *scraping* and less *screeching*.

The RV finally began to move, and everyone cheered.

Zach picked up speed and headed for the exit.

Congratulations were given and high-fives shared until the green van bounced into view. It squealed to a stop directly in front of the exit.

"What do we do?" Piper shouted. "We're blocked!"

Zach gave no answer, but punched the gas harder.

"Zach?!"

They picked up speed ... heading directly for the van.

Piper screamed, "*Zach, what are you—*"

They plowed into the side of the van with a loud *CRASH,* pushing it four or five feet to the side.

Zach shifted the RV into reverse, rolled back several yards, and shifted into first. Again he hit the gas.

"*ZACH!*"

And again they hit the van—this time smashing its front side and spinning it around until it slammed into the wall. Water began spewing out of its radiator immediately. The people inside seemed okay, but their van was definitely not going anywhere.

Everyone cheered as Zach squeezed the RV past the van, gave a wave to the red-haired woman, and bounced onto the street. He gunned it, and they took off, throwing Piper backward. She would have hit the floor had Cody not been there to catch her.

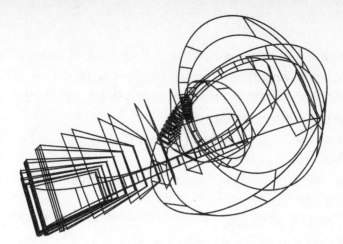

# Chapter Ten

## Wrapping Up

Once they were far enough away, Zach pulled into a gas station to put air back into the tires.

"I'll take care of it," Cody said as he hopped out of the side door.

Piper leaned back in her seat. It had been a long, hard day that had taken its toll on everyone. Well, everyone but Eli. He just sat there beside her, humming away like everything was peachy keen. But it wasn't, not by a long shot.

"Hey, Willard," Zach called from up front. "Any luck on that computer yet?"

"Yes, I believe so," Willard said as he stared at his handheld device.

Piper looked over to him. "What are you doing?"

"I gave him our email address," Zach said. "I wanted him to see if we got anything from Mom or Dad."

"And the answer is an affirmative," Willard said. "It appears you have two messages."

Piper sat up in excitement. "Two messages?"

"Yes, that is correct."

"It appears to have come from an organization entitled The ... Organization."

"The Organization?" Piper asked. "Who are they? What does it say? What do they want?"

"Probably just spam mail," Zach called back.

Willard snorted. "With my latest in software technology? Highly improbable."

"What do they say?" Piper asked.

"Patience, child. Patience." He took a moment, cleared his throat, and finally read the message.

DEAR KIDS,

WE ARE FINE! WE WILL CONTACT YOU SOON. DON'T TRY TO FIND US! IT'S TOO DANGEROUS. DON'T SEND ANY MESSAGES THAT REVEAL YOUR LOCATION. THEY MAY BE CHECKING OUR MAIL.

"They?" Piper asked. "Who's *they?*"

Trying to ignore the interruption, Willard again cleared his throat and continued:

WE WILL FIND YOU. WE WILL CONTACT YOU WHEN WE CAN. PLEASE TAKE CARE OF EACH OTHER. KEEP ELIJAH CLOSE. WE LOVE YOU.

MOM AND DAD

— ROMANS 8:28

Willard looked up. "What is a Romans eight, verse twenty-eight?"

"It's a Bible verse," Zach explained. "Mom and Dad always end their messages with some Bible quote. But what are they saying—that we're just supposed to go on like this?"

There was a moment of silence broken only when Cody opened the door and climbed back inside. "All set to go," he said.

"Right," Piper nodded. "But where?"

"Say what?"

Zach explained. "We can take you and Willard back home, but what are *we* supposed to do?"

"What about the other message?" Piper asked Willard. "You said there were two?"

Willard scrolled down to the second message. Once again he cleared his throat and read.

DEAR KIDS. DISREGARD PREVIOUS MESSAGE. NEED HELP. BEING HELD AT COMPOUND IN MOUNTAINS. COME FOR US. MAKE SURE ELIJAH IS WITH YOU. DIRECTIONS ARE BELOW.

MOM AND DAD

With a heavy sigh, Zach turned forward in the driver's seat, reached for the key, and started up the RV.

"What are you doing?" Piper demanded.

"Mom and Dad need our help," he called back as they pulled from the station.

Piper frowned. "Yeah, but ..."

"But what?" Cody asked.

"That second message doesn't even sound like Mom and Dad."

Willard added, "And there is no Bible reference, like you say they always include."

Silence stole over the RV.

Finally, Zach called back. "It doesn't matter who sent that second message. The point is Mom and Dad are in trouble."

Piper agreed. "And we're the only ones who can help them."

"So what are you going to do?" Cody asked.

"The only thing we can do," Piper answered. "Look for them."

"Way up in the mountains?" Willard asked.

Zach nodded. "If that's what it takes."

"There is a high probability that you may be walking into a trap," Willard warned.

"I know," Zach said. "But like Piper says, what else we can do? We'll just have to be careful."

"Yeah," Piper nodded in thoughtful agreement. "*Very* careful."

●

Monica watched as the tow truck hooked up their van and prepared to take it to a garage for repairs. Her left eye was twitching, her right foot was tapping, and she kept swallowing. Translation: She was on the garage's phone with Shadow Man.

"You ssshall come to the compound immediately," Shadow Man hissed. "Follow the route you think they will take. They are coming here, sssearching for their parentsss. If you misss them on the road, we ssshall grab them here."

"Yes, sir," Monica replied. "There's just one thing."

"Yesss …"

"There's this man. Twice when we came close to nabbing those brats, he appeared from nowhere and blocked us."

There was no answer, only a loud, raspy gasp.

"Sir?"

Still no answer.

"Sir, are you there?"

When the voice returned, it was a harsh whisper. "And ssso it has come to thisss."

"Excuse me?"

"The enemy . . . He is sssending reinforcementsss."

Monica gulped. "Enemy, sir?"

"SSSILENCE!" he shouted. Then more calmly, he continued. "You will sssearch for them as you make your way here. And, thisss time, you will make no more missstakesss."

"Y-yes sir. No mistakes."

"We have no room for failure. Sssoon the boy will be oursss to control or kill as we sssee fit."

Monica gulped harder.

"Sssoon. Very, very ssssssoon."

The Elijah Project
The Enemy Closes In
Bill Myers
with James Riordan
bestselling author

# Chapter One

## The Chase Continues

The tires of the old RV squealed around the turn.

Piper flew across the motor home, slamming hard into the door. "Zach, slow down!"

Of course, her big brother didn't listen. What else was new? But this time he had an excuse. Driving the RV up the winding mountain road was tricky. Especially when people were chasing them.

Especially when those people wanted to kidnap their little brother.

Especially when they had guns.

He took another corner, throwing Piper in the opposite direction. "Zach!"

He grinned, pushing aside his handsome black hair—handsome if you like haircuts that look like they were trimmed by a lawn mower.

Throwing a look out the back window, Piper saw the green van, driven by their pursuers, closing in.

She glanced at six-year-old Elijah. He was sound asleep. Although she loved him dearly, the kid was definitely odd. He seldom, if ever talked, but he always seemed to know things no one else did.

Then there were the miracles—healing a girl in the hospital, raising a puppy from the dead. Of course the family tried to keep the stuff secret, but people always found out.

Which was probably why the bad guys were after them.

Which was probably why their parents had been kidnapped and hidden somewhere in these mountains. Someone very evil was using them as bait. And Piper and Zach were the only ones who could save them.

"What if it's a trap?" Piper had asked as they started out on the journey toward The Operation's headquarters. "What if Mom and Dad didn't send that message wanting us to rescue them?"

"Then it's a trap," Zach shrugged. "What other choice do we have?"

Of course he was right. It was just hard to remember little details like that when you were being thrown around a motor home like a human Ping-Pong ball.

They took another corner, faster and sharper than all the others.

"ZACH!"

●

The driver of the green van was a skinny guy by the name of Silas. He was shouting to his red-haired passenger, Monica. "Are you sure they're going to break down?"

"That's what Shadow Man said."

"Right, but—"

"Has he ever been wrong before?" she asked.

"No, but—"

"Then shut up and keep driving!" (Monica was not exactly the polite type.)

A third voice called from the back. "Shadow Man—he's like my hero."

Silas and Monica rolled their eyes. They always rolled their eyes when Bruno spoke. He was a huge man with a tiny brain.

"Wanna know why?" he asked.

"Why?" Silas said.

"'Cause he brought me and Monica together."

Monica stole a look over her shoulder. As always, the man was all misty-eyed and ga-ga over her.

As always, she felt her stomach churn.

And, as always, she answered in her most pleasant screech. "Put a sock in it!"

"Yes, my sweets." He sighed dreamily. "Whatever you say."

●

The RV gave a loud *clunk*.

"Oh no!" Piper cried "What's that?"

"I don't know." Zach pressed on the gas pedal, but it did no good. *CLUNK! CLUNK!* They were definitely slowing.

"There's a gas station." Piper pointed to the right. "Pull in there."

"And just wait for those creeps to grab Eli?" Zach argued.

CLUNK! CLUNK! CLUNK!

Piper glanced at her little brother, who was now wide awake and looking out the side window. Not only looking, but grinning and waving.

Piper followed his gaze to the road. No one was there.

CLUNK! CLUNK! CLUNK! CLUNK! The engine finally stopped.

Zach shifted the RV into neutral and coasted the rest of the way into the station.

●

"LOOK OUT!" Monica screamed.

Silas looked up just in time to see an old hitchhiker standing in the middle of the road. He hit the brakes. They skidded out of control and swerved, barely missing the old-timer.

"WATCH IT!"

Now they slid toward the guardrail and a 200-foot drop-off.

Silas cranked the wheel hard, and the tires smoked ... until the van hit the rail and bounced back onto the road.

"WHAT WERE YOU DOING?!" Monica demanded.

"I'm trying to keep us alive!"

"You almost got us killed!"

"I'm not the one standing in the middle of the road!"

"The old coot!" Monica looked back over her shoulder. "He could have gotten us all—" She stopped. "Wait a minute, where did he go?"

Silas glanced into the mirror. Try as he might, he could not see the old man.

"Did we, uh, squash him?" Bruno asked.

"I don't think so." Silas started to slow down.

"What are you doing now?" Monica said.

"We better go back and check."

"We're not checking anything!"

"But—"

"If he wants to get hit, that's his business. We got some brats to catch!" Monica turned back to watch the RV in front of them. There was only one problem.

"Where is it?" she asked.

Silas searched the road before them and saw the same thing.

Nothing.

The motor home they'd been chasing all this time was nowhere to be seen. "Where'd it go?" Bruno asked.

"I don't know." Silas frowned. "They were right in front of us a second ago."

"Well, step on it!" Monica shouted. "Don't let them get away!"

●

"Did you see that?" Zach asked. He watched as the green van continued up the highway, passing them and the gas station.

"They didn't even see us!" Piper said. "They were too busy swerving and skidding."

Zach searched the road. "I wonder why."

"Maybe they were trying to miss a deer or something."

Zach shook his head. "No, there was nothing there." He glanced into the mirror to see Elijah sitting in his seat, smiling back at him.

Piper spotted him too. "Looks like the little guy knows something we don't."

Zach nodded and let out a weary sigh. "So what else is new?"

●

Mom and Dad sat chained to opposite walls in the cold, dark room.

"How are you holding up?" Dad asked. His voice was hoarse and cracked from lack of water.

"I just can't stop thinking about the kids," Mom said.

He heard the worry in her voice and nodded. "We just have to ..." He swallowed back the emotion in his voice and tried again. "We just have to be strong."

Outside, there was the rattling of keys. The door creaked open, and a guard just slightly smaller than a semitruck entered the room. "Time to see the boss," he grunted as he stooped to unlock their chains.

"Please ..." Mom's voice quivered. "Not again. There's nothing we can tell him."

"It'll be all right," Dad said. But inside he didn't believe it for a second.

"I just can't face him." Mom began to cry. "The way he burrows into my thoughts with those awful eyes."

"Stop your whining." The guard hoisted each of them to their feet. "It'll be over soon enough." He pushed them into the dimly lit hall. "If you're lucky."

# Chapter Two

## The Plan

"I just feel like we deserted them," Cody said as they entered the cluttered garage.

"*Them?*" Willard, his pudgy friend with curly hair said. "Or *her?*"

"Her, who?" Cody asked.

"Her, *Piper*," Willard answered.

"What are you talking about?" They walked around another one of Willard's failed inventions:

**The Nuclear Powered Dental Flosser**—a giant, two-story machine designed to automatically floss your teeth while you slept. Not a bad idea, except instead of cleaning your teeth, it sort of yanked them out.

"I see the way she looks at you," Willard teased. "Course, it's no big deal 'cause all the girls do that."

"Yeah, right," Cody scoffed.

Willard had to smile. Cody was clueless over his good looks and the effect he had on girls, which is probably why the two of them were still best friends.

"There's only one difference," Willard said.

"What's that?"

"I also see the way *you* look at *her*."

Cody glanced down, embarrassed. "It's just that she …" He caught himself and tried again. "It's just that we're back here, and *they* are all alone in that motor home up in the mountains."

"Not exactly." They stopped in front of another gigantic pile of junk. Willard reached in and dug out a laptop computer along with a pair of night-vision goggles.

"Cool," Cody said. "You get those goggles from the Army?"

Willard shook his head. "It's another one of my inventions."

"Uh-oh …"

"No, listen, these are way cool. Check 'em out." Willard pulled a cable from the pile and began attaching it. "These will let us watch Piper and her brothers wherever they are."

"I hope they work better than your helio-hopper."

"Why's that?"

"'Cause that almost killed us … twice."

"No," Willard insisted. "These are perfectly safe. You just plug them in, like so …" He finished attaching the cable to the computer and then the goggles.

"Willard, I don't think—"

"Then you put them on, like so …" He fitted the goggles over his thick glasses. "Then you enter their email address, like so …" He typed Zach and Piper's email address into the computer.

"Willard, are you sure—"

"And then finally you turn them on, like so." He flipped a switch on the side of the goggles and waited.

Fortunately, nothing happened.

Cody gave a sigh of relief.

Unfortunately, Willard wasn't done. "Maybe there's a short." He looked to the keyboard. "Maybe ... Wait a minute! Of course! I forgot to hit Enter."

"Willard, I really don't—"

He pressed the key, and the goggles lit up like a Christmas tree. Only it wasn't just the goggles. It was also ...

"Willard!" Cody shouted.

That's right, the boy's face now glowed like a nightlight. And his body shook like a bowl of Jell-O on a jack hammer.

"T-t-t-turn i-t-t-t offfff ..." he cried.

"How?" Cody yelled. "Where?!"

"D-d-d-de-leeet-e!" Willard shouted. "Hit-t-t-t d-d-de-lete!"

Cody reached over to the computer and hit the Delete key. Instantly the goggles went off and everything was back to normal.

Well, almost everything ...

It seemed Willard's hair was still smoldering. Actually it wasn't so much hair anymore. Now it was more like smoking peach fuzz.

"Are you okay?!" Cody asked.

Willard pulled off his goggles and sighed. "I hate it when that happens."

●

"Boy, you did a number to this baby." The old mechanic slammed shut the engine compartment to the RV.

Zach and Piper traded nervous looks.

"How much is it going to cost?" Zach asked.

"Well first you got your alternator. That's a hundred and sixty bucks. Then you got your battery. That's gonna be—"

"Whoa, whoa, whoa." Zach held up his hand. "We don't even have the one sixty."

"Then I'd say you got yourself a problem." The mechanic wiped his hands on an oily rag and limped away. Zach and Piper ran to catch up.

"There must be something you can do," Piper said.

"I can let you use my phone to call your folks."

"I wish it was that easy," she mumbled.

The old man blew his nose into the oily rag, then checked it for results. "If I ain't fixin' it, you ain't leavin' it here," he said.

"Right." Zach looked around, trying to figure out what to do.

"Can we get back to you?" Piper asked.

The old-timer shrugged. "If you ain't got the money, you ain't got the money. 'Less, you're expectin' some sorta miracle."

The word touched off an idea in Zach's mind, and he turned to Elijah. As usual, his little brother was clueless—unless you call playing with a caterpillar on a nearby tree having a clue. Still ...

Zach glanced over to the roadside diner next door. "Can we grab a bite to eat before we give you an answer?"

"Suit yourself. Just don't take too long." The mechanic blew his nose again and checked for results. This time he was more pleased.

●

Mom and Dad entered the dark office. In the shadows, a huge man sat behind his desk. They'd seen him before—felt his chilling power.

"Welcome," he hissed.

Mom shifted, trying to get a better look. But no matter how she moved, his face seemed to stay in shadow, even when light hit it.

"What do you want from us?" Dad demanded. His voice sounded strong, but Mom could tell he was terrified. Who wouldn't be?

"SSSILENCCCE!" the man shouted. "I am the one who assksss the quessstionsss." The room grew very, very still. Ever so slowly, he rose from his desk. "Where isss he?"

"You'll get nothing from us." Dad said.

"Really . . . ?"

Mom didn't like the man's tone. She liked it even less when he started toward them. Maybe he walked, maybe he floated. She couldn't tell in the dark.

"Oh, but I will get sssomething from you," he hissed. "If not your cooperation . . . then at leasst their weaknessesss."

"Their weaknesses?" Dad asked.

"Yesss." He arrived and hovered over Mom. She pulled back. "You will tell me their weaknessesss, and I will ussse them."

"What do you mean?" her voice trembled. "Use them for what?"

"Why, to dessstroy them, of courssse." His long fingers shot out and wrapped around her head. She tried to scream but could not find her voice. Her eyes began to shudder.

"Ssshow me," he hissed. "Ssshow me your oldessst."

Before she could stop herself, thoughts of Zach raced through her mind. His sense of humor, his over-inflated ego, his weakness for girls.

"Yesss." The evil voice seemed to come from inside

her head. "Yesss, I ssshall ussse that." Then he started to laugh. It was ugly. Menacing. "Yesss ... yesss ..." His laugh grew louder and louder, filling her head until she collapsed onto the floor and heard nothing at all.

●

"So what do we do?" Piper asked. She and Elijah sat in a booth across from Zach in the diner. "I saw a Help Wanted sign in the window. Maybe I could get a job."

"You don't know how to be a waitress," Zach said.

"I could learn."

"I got something better." Zach pulled his hand from his coat pocket and produced a wadded gum wrapper and their life savings of $1.47.

"Great," Piper groaned. "That'll do us a lot of good."

But Zach wasn't listening. Instead, he turned to Elijah. "So what do you think, little guy?"

Elijah looked at the money and smiled.

Zach held it closer.

"What are you doing?" Piper asked.

"Remember back in the RV how he multiplied the burgers and fries so we had enough to eat?"

"Yeah ..."

"So, if he can multiply burgers and fries, he can multiply money."

"Zach ..."

"What?" He held the money closer. "Come on, fella, do your thing."

"Isn't that kind of ... dishonest?"

"What's dishonest about it?"

At last, Elijah reached for his hand.

"There we go, that's right. Just touch it and ..."

But instead of taking the money, the boy picked up the wadded gum wrapper.

"No, no, no," Zach said. "The money ... we need *money.*"

Elijah looked at him, grinned, and set the paper on the table.

"*No.*" Zach shook the money in his hand. "*This!*"

Elijah began playing with the wrapper.

"*This!* Eli, we need more of THIS!"

But Elijah was too busy playing to hear.

Piper covered her mouth, trying not to laugh. Elijah looked up at her. His eyes sparkled like he understood. Maybe he did.

"Hi, there."

Piper turned to see their waitress. She was about Zach's age, with black hair, black clothes, black fingernail polish, and some major black eyeliner. She was definitely Goth, but underneath all that makeup she was probably cute. And by the way she flirted with Zach, she was definitely interested.

"Can I take your order?"

"Yeah," Zach shrugged. "I guess we'll just ... uh ..." He glanced down at his money. "We'll just split some fries."

"That's it?"

"All we have is a dollar forty-seven."

"But you're hungry, right?"

"Oh yeah, big time."

"Right." She gave him another smile and started scribbling on her pad. "That's three deluxe burgers, three sides of fries, three milkshakes, and one hot apple turnover."

"No, you don't understand. We can't afford—"

She flipped her hair to the side. "I understand perfectly. And what the boss doesn't know won't hurt him."

"What?"

"It's on the house, big guy."

Zach could only stare. Come to think of it, that's all Piper could do too.

The waitress flashed another smile. "It's the least I can do for a hottie like you." She turned and started off. "I'll be back."

Zach broke into a grin and nodded. "Right. We'll, uh, see you soon."

"Zach," Piper whispered, "we can't do that."

"Why not?" Zach said, still impressed with himself.

"Because she's ripping off the restaurant to feed us."

"Oh well." He shrugged.

"Oh well? That's all you can say?"

"Hey, it's not my fault I'm such a hottie."

Piper rolled her eyes and groaned.

## The Enemy Closes In

Softcover • ISBN 9780310711940

Zach meets a runaway who dabbles with the supernatural, and Elijah comes to their aid while another evil force closes in—the foul Shadow Man. But Shadow Man is no match for heavenly forces watching over them.

Available now at your local bookstore!

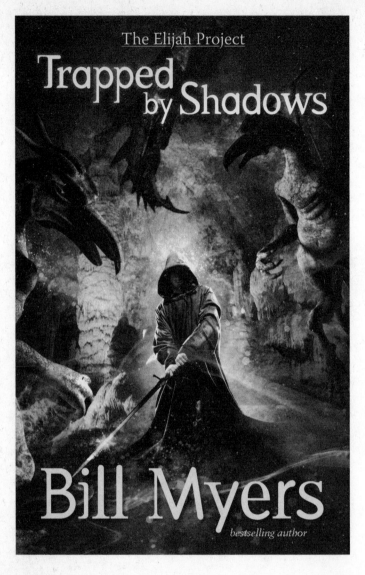

**Trapped by Shadows**
Softcover • ISBN 9780310711957

Elijah is captured, and his family must enter the Abyss to save him. The deeper they plunge into the caves, the greater the danger to them all, but they are not alone. Heaven is on their side.

## Chamber of Lies

Softcover • ISBN 9780310711964

Zach, Piper, and Elijah are reunited with their parents. But when Elijah is lured into the Chamber, he must face the Shadow Man in a battle for his soul. Only heaven can help him now.

**Available now at your local bookstore!**

## NIV Adventure Bible
Softcover • ISBN 9780310715436

In this revised edition of the *NIV Adventure Bible*, kids 9-12 will discover the treasure of God's Word. Filled with great adventures and exciting features, the *NIV Adventure Bible* opens a fresh new encounter with Scripture for kids, especially at a time when they are trying to develop their own ideas and opinions independent of their parents.

**Available now at your local bookstore!**

## NIV Adventure Bible Book of Devotions
By Robin Schmitt
Softcover • ISBN 9780310714477

Get Ready for Adventure!
Grab your spyglass and compass and set sail for adventure! Like a map that leads to great treasure, the *NIV Adventure Bible Book of Devotions* takes kids on a thrilling, enriching quest. This yearlong devotional is filled with exciting fictional stories about kids finding adventure in the real world. Boys and girls will learn more about God and the Bible, and be inspired to live a life of faith—the greatest adventure of all. Companion to the Adventure Bible, the #1 bestselling Bible for kids.

**Available now at your local bookstore!**

# The Star-Fighters of Murphy Street Series

## By Robert West

Introducing the Star-Fighters of Murphy Street: three unlikely young heroes bound for some of the zaniest escapades you can imagine.

### There's a Spaceship in My Tree: Episode I

Softcover • ISBN 9780310714255

Newly arrived from California, thirteen-year-old Beamer MacIntyre feels like an alien in this bizarre Midwestern town. Strangest of all is the spaceship-shaped tree house in his yard.

### Attack of the Spider Bots: Episode II

Softcover • ISBN 9780310714262

Star-Fighters Beamer, Ghoulie, and Scilla follow a strange clanking sound in their cave labyrinth and stumble onto a screaming one-eyed monster that chases them into a huge cavern enclosing a fully animated miniature world.

### Escape From the Drooling Octopod! : Episode III

Softcover • ISBN 9780310714279

The Star-Fighters, under attack from pink goblins and Molgotha, a drooling giant octopod, must save a girl locked in a "pink palace."

**Available now at your local bookstore!**